HERNE THE HUNTER

'Draw, damn you!'

The kid screamed at the top of his voice, hand slapping down, body ducking and beginning to twist, knees bending. Herne reacting like a prairie rattler. Hand blurring for the butt of the forty-five. So much faster than the boy. Three fingers around the polished wood, drawing the gun easily from the greased leather. Thumb pulling back on the hammer, triple-clicking into place. Index finger snug and tight around the thin trigger of the pistol...

ALSO IN THIS SERIES

HERNE THE HUNTER

1: White Death
2: River of Blood
3: The Black Widow
4: Shadow of the Vulture
5: Apache Squaw
6: Death in Gold
7: Death Rites
8: Cross-Draw
9: Massacre!
10: Vigilante!

and published by Corgi Books

Herne The Hunter 11: Silver Threads

John J. McLaglen

CORGI BOOKS
A DIVISION OF TRANSWORLD PUBLISHERS LTD

HERNE THE HUNTER 11: SILVER THREADS
A CORGI BOOK 0 552 11130 9

First publication in Great Britain

PRINTING HISTORY

Corgi edition published 1979

Corgi Books are published by Transworld Publishers Ltd, Century House, 61-63 Uxbridge Road, Ealing, London, W5 5SA

Made and printed in Great Britain by
C. Nicholls & Company Ltd,
The Philips Park Press, Manchester

With thanks for all their efforts, this one is for Mike Stotter and Dave Whitehead – a couple of desperadoes waiting for the train.

'Darling, I am growing old,
Silver threads among the gold
Shine upon my brow today;
Life is fading fast away.'

From *Silver Threads Among The Gold* by
Eben Rexford, 1848-1916.

CHAPTER ONE

Wild Rose City, in the Dakota Territory, in the late spring of eighteen hundred and eighty-five was one of the most beautiful places in the whole of America.

Centred on its main street that ran parallel to the foaming Clearwater River, its neat frame houses rose primly towards the crest of the hill, where the graveyard spread among shady trees, the orderly white markers in rows along tended paths.

The silver mine that had brought prosperity to that part of the Black Hills was situated at Mount Morgoth, a couple of miles to the west of the town. The mining camp was at the base of the waste tip, with its saloons and its wild women.

There was nothing like that in Wild Rose. Of course there was a saloon. *The Rich Nugget* it was called, and it was run by an ex-cavalry sergeant called Quincannon. Though no lady ever went there, naturally, she would have been quite safe. It was a most respectable establishment, and perfectly reflected the moral tone of the entire town.

Nor were there drunken whores dangling over balconies flaunting their naked bodies to try and tempt innocent youth from the paths of righteousness.

Since it was recognised there were occasions that some men needed to go to a private place and relieve there the beastly tensions that they could not insult their dear wives with, there was a house of assignation in Wild Rose. A neat house on a side road off the High Street. Like the other neat houses. The only clue to its aura of discreet immorality the muted crimson oil lamp that burned at the side of the porch during the evenings. Only to be promptly extinguished at midnight by order of the town council.

If you were sober and orderly then Wild Rose City welcomed you. If you weren't then by thunder but you'd better just be passing through!

Sheriff Daley could be seen most days sitting in a worn rocker outside the jail, boots rested on the rail, watching to see if he could be of assistance to any lost child or elderly lady who wanted someone to help her across the dusty street with a load of shopping. He was a tall man, slightly running to fat. Little eyes like black beads almost buried in the doughy wrinkles of his face.

Most folks smiled when they passed Sheriff Daley.

It was a good thing to do.

Sheriff Daley liked folks who smiled at him.

The country had been Republican since the War, and Wild Rose City was no exception. Abe, and Andy Johnson. Ulysses S. Grant and Rutherford Hayes. Poor murdered James Garfield and on with the current President, Chester A. Arthur.

Republican through and through.

Sheriff Daley was a Republican.

He was also the nephew of the Misses Sowren. Miss Lily Sowren. And her younger sister, Miss Liza Sowren. And they were the power behind Wild Rose. Their father had found the lode with its rich silver veins spreading through the Dakotas. Opening up Mount Morgoth before the War. Keeping it going through the fighting. Starting to build Wild Rose to give decent folks somewhere nice to live away from the stench and death of the mine and its brawling workers.

Dying quietly in his sixties while reading the lesson in church. Handing the whole town over, lock, stock and barrel, to his daughters. Lil and Liza.

Liza had been married for a couple of years, but there wasn't anyone in the town could recall much of the husband. He'd been a Mister Springstein. A pale little man from New Jersey. He'd come west, bringing money to help the Mount Morgoth Mine out at a time when it needed capital. He'd lived in the big Sowren house up on the top of the hill, overlooking that neat cemetery. Liza had duly been delivered of three children. All male. One dead and two living. After that it seemed as if Mister Springstein had done all that God intended him to do. He succumbed to a fever in eighteen fifty-six and was buried in an imposing tomb overlooking the slopes of the small town and the white ribbon of the Clearwater.

Despite her marriage folks carried on calling Liza Sowren 'Miss Sowren', just as if the marriage had never happened. Miss Lily and Miss Liza ruled the town.

On this particular Sunday morning they were walking together. Promenading steadily homewards from church, nodding to those of their acquaintances among the town's people that merited their recognition.

The sun was baking down from a sky of cloudless blue, and it was possible to hear the distant rumbling of the river as it dived and whirled among the rocks, carried to their ears on the back of a gentle wind.

'It is a most beautiful morning, Sister Lily,' said Eliza.

'Indeed it is, Sister Eliza,' replied Lily Sowren, adjusting the angle of her parasol so that the rays of the sun didn't strike directly on her pale cheeks.

They were an odd couple. Almost humorous to look at. Not that anyone in Wild Rose City would ever have laughed at them. Not when you considered that Liza's eldest son,

Joab, ran the bank, and held mortgage deeds on just about all the properties in the town. And that her other son, Gawain, owned the hardware store. And the dry goods store. And the livery stable. And the food stores. In fact Gawain Sowren owned all the stores, and he sold a lot on credit.

Any newcomers to the town used to wonder how it was that Miss Sowren could have two sons, and why they were called with her surname rather than the father's. But when you encountered the Misses Sowren you didn't wonder any longer.

Their influence didn't end with their sons. There'd been their father's brother, Myron Sowren. He'd lived away from town for most of his life and it had been a surprise when three tall young men appeared in the town. Myron had had a daughter, who'd married a man from Vermont named Daley. There'd been three boys born before cholera had wiped out the parents while they were on their way west with a wagon train to start a new life.

Destitute and with no other kin, the boys had come to their aunts in the Dakotas. Charity didn't flow through the town streets like milk and honey, and there were a few privately raised eyebrows when the sisters took the boys in. Built them a house not far down the hill from their own and set about establishing them in business on their own account.

That had been long years back, and those tall young men were now middle-aged. Sturdy, and still tall, but all three running to fat.

Sheriff Matthew Daley.

Marcus Daley, who ran *The Rich Nugget* saloon.

And there was Julius Daley, fattest of the three, and nominally owner of the discreetly run house with the red lamp outside. Julius was also the mayor of Wild Rose City.

The rest of the town council was easy enough to work out.

Miss Lily Sowren, Miss Eliza Sowren, Joab Sowren, Gawain Sowren, Matthew Daley and Marcus Daley.

Surprisingly there were a couple of people on the council that weren't kin. Doctor George G. Hillman was the town physician. A position of such status that it guaranteed him a place on the council.

There were tongues that wagged in private – very much in private – and said that if there had been a Sowren or a Daley with any kind of medical qualification, then Doctor Hillman wouldn't have got within a hundred miles of the council.

The other person on the council was the mine manager. Robert Zimmerman. A skinny, curly-headed man from Hibbing, Minnesota. A brilliant mining engineer who had been brought in by the ladies when there was a whisper that the Mount Morgoth lode was running thin. Under Zimmerman's guidance the rumour had remained just a rumour.

But everyone else in Wild Rose was just a bit-player compared to the ladies.

Strolling home through the Sunday sun.

Their shadows on the swept sidewalk revealing the grotesque contrast in their appearances. One shadow that was round and squat, like a huge ball. The other like a shadow in late evening when the sun sinks low in the west. An elongated shadow, looking like a bundle of narrow sticks thrown carelessly together to make a human shape. Stretched and thin.

Lily was the fat one. Grossly fat, her body wobbling like a vast milk pudding, barely contained in her expensive clothes. You could almost hear her stays creaking with the strain of holding in such a bulk. Her face was a succession of layers of chins, cascading down her dimpled cheeks like the terraced slopes of an Asiatic village.

Despite her size, Lily was always immaculately dressed,

in the latest fashions. Copied from smart papers from back East, adapted for her by a little woman who specialised in dressmaking. Pink was her favourite colour. And that Sunday morning Miss Lily Sowren was clothed from top to toe in pink. Her parasol was pink, fringed with pink lace and tassels. Her silk dress, with flounced sleeves and lace at the bosom, was also pink. The palest of coral pinks. Except for the darker patches spread around both armpits. Despite all of their wealth and power there was nothing Lily could do to stop herself sweating. Her shoes were pink, tied with pink ribbons. Their toes peeking coyly out from underneath the shapely tent of her dress. Not that Lily could see her toes. Except for an occasional glimpse in a mirror, Lily Sowren hadn't seen her own toes for better than thirty years.

Just as Lily resembled an elegantly costumed whale, so her sister was like a smartly turned-out xylophone. Apart from their mutual desire to always look respectable, they were complete physical opposites.

Lily was short and stout.

Eliza was a prim streak of nothingness. She topped six feet in height, but if she stood sideways on to you it was hard to see her. Behind their closed doors folks in Wild Rose said she had to run around in the shower to get herself wet.

Her nose was like a steep slice of granite, sharp enough to cut through cheese, with her eyes perched uneasily on either side of it, glinting at the world from her towering height. Her favourite hue was purple, and her parasol to the tips of her buttoned boots were all shades of that colour.

'Here comes Father MacGonagall, sister,' said Eliza, squinting under the dangling lace of her purple parasol at the approaching figure.

'Looks to be in something of a rush, sister,' replied Lily

Sowren, stopping in her tracks, reaching up with a pink-gloved hand to wipe away a trickle of perspiration from the shadow of a moustache that adorned her upper lip.

The priest of Wild Rose City was a willowy young man, barely in his twenties. The son of a merchant banker from Des Moines, Father Angus MacGonagall had preferred the idea of being a poet, but his verse had met with little enthusiasm back in Des Moines. So it had been the clergy as the only other possibility. His father had helped to build the church part way up Main Street on the condition that his son should inherit the living in perpetuity. The Misses Sowren were not ladies to look gift horses in the teeth and had accepted gladly, seeing in the pliable fabric of the young priest nothing that would check their tight hold on Wild Rose City and everything and everyone in it.

And Banker MacGonagall had thought it a small price for him to be rid of his whining son for good, pattering his own prayer each night that nothing would happen to make Angus give up his vocation and quit the Dakotas. He need not have worried. The priest was incapable of ever making such an important decision for himself.

'Miss Lily. Miss Eliza. Beautiful morning, is it not?'

He had the habit of greeting people from a great distance, necessitating the need to reply long before you were within normal range. This frequently meant that by the time you were actually face to face with him, you had exhausted the topic of conversation.

'Morning, Father,' chorused the two elderly ladies.

'Hope it isn't something too taxing for us, sister,' muttered Lily.

'Of course, dear,' replied Eliza. 'You want to get home so that you can retire to your room and pursue your private literary task for Sunday.'

The fat face wrinkled into an expression that might almost

have been anger. If it had been possible to imagine why such an innocent remark between sisters could have produced that feeling.

'Have you heard the news, ladies?' shouted the young priest, flushed from having pursued the sisters all the way from the church.

'What news could that be, Father MacGonagall?' asked Miss Lily Sowren.

'Not bad news, I trust,' added Miss Eliza Sowren, glaring at him down her pointed beak, like a vulture considering whether there was enough meat on its victim to justify bothering with an attack.

He was coming closer, battling up the dusty hill while the Misses Sowren waited patiently for him, waving away an arrant mosquito that didn't realise what exalted flesh it was trying to attack.

'Another robbery,' he yelped, running out of breath while still thirty paces off.

'Another, Father MacGonagall? Why, that is too awful to even contemplate.'

'Indeed it is, Sister Eliza,' wheezed Lily. 'I pray to the sweet Lord Jesus that it was not one of our consignments and that no soul was hurt.'

The hot breath burning in his throat like stretched wire, the priest at last joined them, enabling them all to carry on the conversation in something approaching a normal tone of voice.

'It was awful, I am told. I learned it from the son of Mister Hempstead, the clerk at the dry goods store. He'd been riding out to visit his married sister, Lee-Anne. The girl who was wed in my own church to the eldest boy of . . .'

Lily held up a hand so fat that it resembled a bunch of stumpy pink bananas and checked the garrulous young man.

'That is enough, Father MacGonagall. My sister and I

truly have no wish to stand here on this most beautiful morning and listen while you allow your conversation to ramble unchecked along the highways and the byways. Kindly adhere only to the facts.'

'I'm so sorry, Miss Sowren,' turning to face the other sister, squinting up at her great height. 'I'm sorry, Miss Sowren.'

'Get on with it, Father MacGonagall,' snapped Eliza, irritably.

'Of course. Of course.'

It was a sadly familiar story.

A story that was being repeated every few weeks or months at many of the silver mines that dotted the Dakota Territory.

In the late summer of eighty-four there'd been the first. The Crippled Star Mine, thirty miles to the north of Wild Rose. Seven weeks later came the second. The Old Number One Mine at Clarkstown, just eleven miles west. Wind Creek Mine and Thunder Creek followed. The attacks on the wagons separated by only nine days.

And every time the attacks followed the same pattern. A wagon, often well guarded, picked off at a place where it should have been safe. Always stopped in its tracks, despite its being escorted by as many as eight armed men. Never much sign of resistance. It was damned odd. Almost as if they'd been stopped by friends and then gunned down in cold blood.

But nobody knew what happened.

Dead men don't do a whole lot of talking.

There was talk that it was ghosts. That maybe the old Dutchman had come gibbering up from the lost mother lode of the Superstitions, hunting men down for revenge. But there's not a ghost around could make off with something in the region of one hundred and ninety thousand dollars worth of the finest silver ore in the Dakotas. In eight different raids, spread over six months.

The local sheriffs had done what they could. Sheriff Daley had ridden out himself with a posse to lend a hand. There'd been a federal marshal drafted in. Even a couple of boys from the Pinkerton Detective Agency. Despite their motto of being 'The eye that never sleeps', the Pinkertons came and went and the robberies continued. It was one of their few failures.

The Reverend Angus MacGonagall stammered out the story of the latest robbery under the watchful eyes of the two ladies. The same as the others. Five men shot down. Bringing the total death toll up to over thirty. It was becoming difficult for the owners of the silver mines to find men prepared to ride shotgun on the wagons any more. Even up at Mount Morgoth there was a distinct shortage of volunteers for the job.

'That all, Reverend?' asked Lily, swatting away a swarm of small flies.

'Well . . .' he said, hesitantly.

'Well what, Minister?' said Eliza, peering down at him with the sort of expression that is normally reserved for something you find on the bottom of your shoe.

'We . . . that is . . . me and a few other folks . . . was wonderin' if we ought to try and do something before our silver gets hit as well.'

The sisters looked at each other for a moment, and the priest had the feeling he'd had before with the Misses Sowren. The feeling that they somehow managed to talk to each other without speaking a word.

'You feel we should hire a shootist. Is that what you are endeavouring to say to us, Minister MacGonagall? Is that it?'

'Well, Ma'am, it might . . .'

Lily suddenly smiled at him, and he positively melted with relief in the warmth. 'The council have thought about this, Mister MacGonagall. You can rest assured that we are not the sort of people who would risk the livelihood of this town and all our many friends.'

'Indeed, sister, that is so. And Amen to that, say I,' interrupted Eliza. 'Though the idea of having to hire us a paid gunman is repugnant, it is the lesser of the evils that confronts us.'

'We are old ladies, Minister,' said Lily, waiting for the contradiction from the priest, and freezing off her smile when it was slow in coming.

'No you . . .'

'Indeed we are, Minister. I am something past my sixtieth year, and my sister is a mite older. We are simply two gentle people, with no concept of the world and its wickedness.'

Both of the Misses Sowren placed their gloved hands together in a pious expression of benevolence, while Father MacGonagall nodded sagely at them.

'So we have taken the necessary steps to procure ourselves a man who will come and save us from the hazards of malefactors.'

'That is damned fine news, ladies and . . .'

'Reverend!!' snapped Lily, her jowls quivering with righteous indignation, the crack in her voice loud enough to raise dust at fifty paces.

'What?'

'Your language, Minister. That is what,' replied Eliza, glowering at him across the flying buttress of her nose.

'We are not used to such talk in our home. Nor here in Wild Rose City,' added Lily, nodding in agreement with her sister. 'There may be silver threads among the gold of our hair, but that does not mean we can be treated with such blatant disrespect.'

'Indeed not, sister,' agreed Eliza.

The poor young man stammered and blushed, wishing himself a hundred miles away from the Black Hills, mumbling his apologies to the daunting duo. Wringing his hands in anguish, knowing that neither of the sisters would allow his slip of the tongue to go unremembered.

'I cannot say how sorry I am, ladies ... Please forgive me for ... I know well enough how chastely you rule your lives and ...'

'That is enough, Reverend,' said Lily firmly. 'To err is human and to forgive is divine. You have erred and we have forgiven you. Now we must go home to continue our devotions on this Sabbath in the privacy of our home. We bid you good-day, Mister MacGonagall.'

With an icy nod they dismissed him from their presence, watching him as he walked quickly off down the Main Street of Wild Rose, towards the clear rushing river. Striding along between the rows of trim houses.

Eliza turned to Lily with a thin-lipped smile at their encounter. 'Know what, sister?'

'What, sister?'

'The priest there. The Goddammed son-of-a-bitch don't have the balls of a bastard butterfly!!'

CHAPTER TWO

Jedediah Travis Herne sat in a nameless saloon in a small town in another part of the Dakotas, sipping moodily at a glass of warm beer, looking at the cable that lay on the stained and chipped table in front of him. Wondering what to do about it.

'Herne the Hunter' was what men called him. It was a name he'd earned over many bloody years of riding hard and shooting first. The smell of black powder smoke was never out of his nostrils and the shadow of death hung at his shoulder.

He was now forty-one years old. A good age for any man out West. For a man who'd lived by the quickness of his gun since the age of fifteen, it was close to a miracle.

Living was the mistakes you didn't make, was what he used to say. Herne hadn't made many mistakes in his life. The one that he had made wasn't the sort of thing you could see coming.

Three years back he'd left his young wife, Louise, while he went into Tucson to get supplies. The little homestead should have been safe enough in the normal run of things. They'd been married only three years, and his young bride had managed to do the impossible. Persuade one of the most notorious guns on the frontier to hang up his weapons.

Life had been looking good for Jed.

Until that day.*

* For the details of Herne's return to the killing trail, see *White Death*, first book in this series, available from Corgi Books.

Now he was alone again, with a lot of killing behind him, and only more death to look forward to. Most of the men he'd ever ridden with were dead. Long dead. Billy and Jesse. Wes. So many of them. Past counting.

The bar-keep watched the tall stranger, trying to find a tag for him. There was something about him that invited caution.

Herne was aware of the interest in him, and he looked up at the fat man behind the bar. Who immediately pretended a great involvement in something he'd just excavated from his left nostril. Jed grinned at him, taking another thoughtful swallow of the beer. Reading the cable one more time.

The bar-keep shivered. Whoever he was, he sure as Hell hoped he wasn't in town for long. There was something to him. He'd been around saloons long enough to get to smell it out. Despite his age, this man was a killer. The keep would have sworn away his month's wages on it.

He figured him at past forty. Standing a little over six feet. Broad with it. Long black hair, streaked with grey at the temples and over the ears. Dressed in a shabby set of clothes covered in trail dust. Colt Peacemaker strapped low on the right thigh. Cutaway rig for a fast draw. Butt of the pistol polished and shining in a greased holster. The way some kids did it who wanted folks to think they were mean shootists. Trying to make an impression. Didn't look to the bar-keep as if the stranger gave a damn for the impression he left. He'd just come in from the telegraph office an hour back, ordering himself a beer and a chaser. Sitting quiet with a white telegraph form in front of him, every now and then picking it up and reading it through.

As if he didn't know what to make of it.

*

Herne couldn't make up his mind.

There were law-officers all across the country who knew Herne the Hunter was in business, and he'd cabled one to find out if there was any work for him. A sheriff who'd helped him some in the past. And now there was this reply.

'*Town council Wild Rose City, Dakota Territory, need top gun as guard silver shipments. Good money and keep. See Misses Sowren soon as possible.*'

Herne had queried the word 'Misses', wondering if it was an error, but the clerk had told him it wasn't. Meant there was two of them.

He could use some dollars fast. But working for a council meant shop-keepers and men with white collars and yellow streaks down their backs. And run by women! It took some thinking on.

Over the years there'd been some strange jobs.*

The bartender broke into his chain of memories, calling across the empty room.

'How 'bout 'nother beer, Mister?'

Herne looked up at him, staring through the smoky dust that hung in the air of even the cleanest saloons. Like an eternal mist, with the beams of the sun breaking through the dirty windows at the front of the building, strung through the saloon like stripes of pale gold. Above the bar there was a badly painted picture. A florid lady with yellow hair displaying charms that were so ample that they couldn't have been painted from life. Carrying that kind of load on her chest, Herne doubted whether she could even have managed to sit up. Someone had used her well displayed private parts for knife practice and the canvas all around the top of her thighs was scarred and torn.

* For all of these adventures, read the earlier titles in the exciting saga of Herne the Hunter, listed at the front of this book, all available from Corgi Books.

'I'll take one more.'

It would help to wash out the dirt from his throat, and maybe ease away some of the dark memories that kept returning to haunt him.

'Chaser?'

'No.'

He couldn't afford the shot of whiskey. Not if he wanted to pay for a night's stabling for his stallion and a bed out back for himself. The handful of coins jingled in his pants' pocket as he shifted in the seat. His eye again catching the pencilled lettering on the telegraph form.

Work for a council. And a handful of damned women.

He looked up as the keep waddled over and planted the glass down on the table. Letting beer spill over the top and form a puddle in front of him.

'Sorry, Mister,' said the man, in the sort of voice that showed he didn't care much either way.

'You could be,' said Herne, deliberately dropping the money in the spilled beer.

'Hey! You didn't have no call for that.'

There'd been times when Herne would have picked up the brewing quarrel. Even maybe pushed it as far as it would go. Just to fight off the boredom of being a hired shootist. But he was getting older and he let the bar-keep walk back across the saloon.

Calling out after him.

'Hey!'

'What is it, Mister?'

'Had a friend down in El Paso. Spent the night in a Mex whore-house down there. Prettiest little ten year old dark-eyed girl you ever seen. Just startin' to bud. Five more years she'd have bloomed and rotted away. But right then she was the prize of the place. Five dollars American for a night with her.'

The bar-keep was interested now, in spite of himself. Standing halfway across the room, holding the wet coins in his fingers. Watching as Herne lifted the glass and drank.

'This friend of mine was a funny guy. Time came to go and settle up. Got himself dressed in his best clothes. Fancy dudes. Shouts out to the old lady runnin' the joint he don't have no money.'

'You there?'

'Sure. Outside waiting for him. Heard the yellin' and that. Loads of them bastards runnin' in with knives. Sayin' they're goin' to cut off my friend where it hurts. Screaming and a couple of shots. Then he appears. At the window on the second floor.'

He drained the glass, putting it back down on the table, then edging it over, eyes never leaving the bar-tender's face, pushing it off so it shattered on the floor. Reaching down very casually and flicking the leather thong off the top of the hammer on the Colt, readying it in case it was needed.

It wasn't.

The bar-keep had seen enough to know that a broken glass wasn't worth getting killed for.

'I yelled for him to jump, and he did. Clean into the middle of the biggest heap of shit you ever did see. Must have been the midden for the whole damned quarter of town. Covered in dust so he didn't see what it was until he was off and flyin' into it. Must have been ten feet deep. He vanished and I figured that was it. Couldn't seem to like the idea of divin' in after him. Then he appears. I tell you, he was covered. Shit in his hair and eyes and mouth. Just plain covered. He looked up at me, eyes white in the mess that soaked his face. Know what he said?'

'No, sir. I don't.'

Herne stood up and pocketed the cable, without even looking at it again.

'He said: "There sure must be somethin' more in life than this." So long.'

And he was gone.

It took Jed Herne three days of hard riding to get to Wild Rose. Beautiful spring mornings, off as soon as dawn lightened the eastern sky. Pushing the stallion on through the green days, stopping off at noon for an hour's rest. Watering the animal and eating a frugal meal himself. Riding on through into the pink evenings.

It was late afternoon on the third day when he heard the sound of the Clearwater River surging through the rocky gorge that ran alongside Wild Rose City. Reining in the horse and sitting back in the saddle with a sigh of contentment.

It had been a hard ride. All along the trail he'd been hearing about the robberies of the silver shipments. There was hardly a large mine within a hundred miles of Wild Rose that the bandits hadn't hit. Snatching finest ore.

And that was the puzzling thing for Jed. He knew a little about mining. Man couldn't spend more than half a lifetime out West without picking up some kind of knowledge. And he couldn't understand why the robbers were picking up ore. Why not wait until it had been through processing and smelting and then take the bullion? Easier to get rid of. Much easier. Whoever the criminals were, they must have some kind of access to a lot of mining and processing equipment. Maybe even be in league with an honestly run plant. That was a thought to play around with.

It was the prettiest town that Herne could ever remember seeing.

He'd passed the Mount Morgoth Mine a couple of miles back, wrinkling his nose at the chemical stench that came billowing from it in noxious clouds, darkening the sun and veiling the blue of the sky. He could understand why the first owner had built his home well away from the source of his wealth. Mister Sowren had chosen well.

The little houses unrolled up the hill, topped by a big white frame mansion that Herne guessed rightly must belong to the ladies named in the cable. Right next to a tree-fringed graveyard that bore no resemblance at all to most of the Boot Hills that Jed had seen. Folks in frontier towns didn't care that much for burying strangers and graves were holes scratched in the dust. With a wooden marker if anyone had the inclination to whittle one and daub on a name and a date.

But Wild Rose City wasn't a bit like that. There was a church. A saloon that looked clean and quiet. Couple of side streets with a livery stable on the corner of one of them. Handful of stores.

From where Herne sat the town looked like something out of a rich little girl's nursery. Almost too good to be true.

Herne had only a couple of dollars left and he went straight to the saloon, leaving his horse tethered to the white rail outside. As he walked up the steps he had the prickling feeling that he was being watched and he stopped in his tracks. It was a feeling that you learned not to ignore. That way you kept living.

Slow and easy, Herne turned round, seeing that it was a lawman. Lying back in a rocking-chair, feet propped up. Just staring at him. Biggish man. Not as fit, maybe, as he thought he was.

That was Jed's first impression.

Waving a hand to him. 'Morning, Sheriff.'

'You come over here, boy,' was the reply, with a slow gesture of the hand.

Despite his experience and age, Jed sometimes found his hair-trigger temper hard to control. Being called like that in the middle of a strange town was one of those times. But he thought about the couple of dollars and he swallowed hard. Walking over and standing in front of the lawman, balanced easily on the balls of his feet. Feeling the afternoon sun warm on the back of his neck.

Sensing a challenge to his authority, Sheriff Daley levered himself out of the chair, looking at the tall stranger with distaste. The old guy hadn't smiled at him. Sheriff didn't take to folks like that.

'Wild Rose don't warm to saddle-bums, Mister,' he said. Measuring out the words as if he was going to have to account for them all at the end of the month.

'I can bet on that, Sheriff,' replied Herne. Noting the scatter-gun bucketed at the lawman's hip. Lazy man's weapon. Doesn't take any skill to blow a person in half with a sawn-off heavy twelve-gauge.

'You're kind of an old man to be wearin' that pistol low on the hip, ain't you?'

Herne put the sheriff at about his own age. Wondering if he might ask whether he wasn't too old for a scatter-gun on the hip. Deciding not to.

'I didn't hear you reply to that, boy.'

'Didn't say anything, Sheriff.'

'Maybe you better talk a whiles. Like tellin' me who you are and what the Hell you're doin' foulin' up a clean street with your dirt?'

'I'm here after a job.'

'Job. Might be somethin' cleanin' out the shit-house round back of the saloon. That's 'bout all I figure you as bein' fit for.'

'Matter of opinion, Sheriff.'

'My opinion, boy. My damned opinion!'

'You're entitled to that.'

The lawman's right hand was edging on down towards the stock of the scatter-gun. And a vein at the centre of his forehead was beginning to throb in anger.

'I'm Sheriff Daley, boy. You heard of me?'

'Can't say I have.'

'I run this town.'

Jed fired off a long shot. 'I heard that the Misses Sowren ran Wild Rose.'

There was a silence like someone had broken wind in a cathedral. Then Daley cleared his throat. 'That's true enough, boy. They're my aunts. You heard of them?'

'Way I understand it, I've come to work for them. Guarding some silver.'

'Holy shit!' He looked quickly round as if he was worried someone might have heard the expletive. 'Old man like you couldn't guard his ass-hole with both hands.'

'Some might not agree, Sheriff,' replied Herne, keeping his voice mild and his fingers clear of the Colt.

'I don't believe I caught your name, did I?'

Jed noticed that the 'boy' had disappeared. The first indication of the magic that the name of the sisters could work in the town.

'Didn't throw it you, Sheriff. But it's Herne. Jedediah Herne.'

There was a look of bewilderment as Sheriff Daley struggled to remember where he'd heard the name. Then it came back to him with the chilling rush of a flash flood.

'Herne the Hunter! You're . . .' Suddenly the gun was out of the holster, the twin barrels gaping at Jed. 'You better let slip that belt real easy, Herne. Jesus! I heard years back you was dead. Some shootin' with that guy with the razor.'

'Josiah Hedges. Man they call "Edge". Hell, no. He's

alive and kickin' and so am I. Maybe both a spell older. But still around.'

'I see that. And you come ridin' in here cool and like you own Wild Rose. Come on! Get that damned belt off before I slice you clean through the guts.'

'Your aunts wouldn't like that, Sheriff. Seein' as I've ridden a long way to come and help them out.'

Daley was confused. He knew that Lily and Eliza had sent out for a gunman to help them. But he was certain sure they had no idea what they'd gone and gotten hold of. Herne the Hunter. That was bad news.

The worst news.

'I guess ... Look, Herne. Maybe I'll give you another chance.'

Jed spat in the dirt, looking up at the ponderous lawman. 'Come on Sheriff. Don't piss on my boots and then tell me it's rainin'.'

'By God ...' The hammers on the shot-gun clicked back. 'Don't you think you ...'

Herne started to turn away, ignoring Daley's anger. 'You don't tell me where I can meet the ladies, then I'll go find someone who can. And I'll tell them the way you greeted me to their town, Sheriff.'

'Just wait on there,' he called after him. 'Wait on and don't be so damned hasty.'

'You change your mind, Sheriff?'

'Yeah. Look, I'll go up the house and tell Miss Lily and Miss Liza that you've come. They'll want me to see ... want to meet you. Maybe with the rest of the council. You go in *The Rich Nugget* and get yourself some of that dust out of your throat. Charge it to me. Fellow runs the saloon's my brother, Marcus. I got to go.'

Herne watched him as he hurried off up the hill towards

the big house, and went on into the saloon, letting the bats-wing doors slam shut behind him.

If he'd waited, he'd have seen that the Sheriff stopped before he reached the Sowren mansion, and dived off down a side street, with the look on his face of a man with a very urgent mission to carry out.

CHAPTER THREE

'Ten dollars a day. Your keep at three meals a day. No liquor. Bed for the night. And your ammunition. For a period of at least three weeks. After such date both parties are free to reconsider their positions. How does that suit you, Mister Herne?'

He nodded. 'Real fine, Miss Sowren. I start right now?'

'As soon as you like. But perhaps you would prefer to wait until the morning. It will be fully dark within the hour.'

He glanced to the opposite side of the long table to the other Miss Sowren. The fat one. Miss Lily.

'Fine with me. I can start by asking around just in case anyone's gotten any information or thoughts on the robberies.'

This time it was Eliza who spoke. 'I think you will find nobody knows a thing, Mister Herne. If anyone had such information, you can be quite certain that they would have brought it either to me or to my sister.'

'Quite right, sister,' agreed Lily, nodding her head so hard that Herne feared some of her chins might come adrift from their moorings and splatter all over the oak table.

The meeting had gone well enough. Though he wondered why it had taken so long to get everyone there. It had been nearly six before he'd finally been introduced to the sisters and the rest of the family and council.

While they talked to him about the robberies, Herne had

sat still and quiet, watching and listening. Forming his impressions. Listing a few questions to himself.

He'd never met anyone quite like Lily and Eliza. They came on like a couple of sweet little old ladies, but everything pointed to a different reality. For one thing, neither of them could be called 'little'. There was something else. Both of them spoke as if their mouths were filled with sugared plums, but there was steel behind it all. A hardness that Herne's experienced eyes didn't miss. You didn't get to run a mining town for as long as they had and as tightly as they did, without being exceptional characters.

The Misses Sowren looked like being the toughest bosses he'd ever had. He'd asked what happened to any robbers he might catch. The question seemed to worry them, then Lily had smiled deep in the rolls of fat.

'Leave them to us, Mister Herne. Eliza and I will do what is necessary, with the help of our family and our friends.'

He bet they would, too.

Both of the sons were typically close-lipped business-men. Joab and Gawain. The banker and the store-owner. Both cast from the same mould. Though they were the sons of skinny Eliza, they had inherited the tendency to fatness of their aunt. Both shook hands with Jed in a way that showed what they thought about hiring a gunman. Both wiping their hands clean after with a white linen 'kerchief.

Marcus and Julius Daley were also of similar build. Both tallish men in their thirties. Both leaning towards chubbiness like their older brother Matthew, the Sheriff. Herne was told about Marcus running the saloon, but he wasn't clear at first about what Julius did. Apart from being the mayor of Wild Rose City.

It was Doctor Hillman who told him. Hissing out of the corner of his mouth when they were alone for a few moments in a corner of the church hall, where the meeting was held.

'Cat-house, owner. Runs the sporting-house, Mister Herne. Six lovely clean girls. Could take your grandmother there without fear of offence.'

The other outsider on the council was the one that most interested Jed. One who had a large question mark against his name.

What was Robert Zimmerman so damned frightened about? So frightened that he nearly dropped the cup of tea that one of the Misses Sowren's servant girls handed him. When he met Herne he looked everywhere except at Jed, his handshake as warm as a dead moth.

The ladies were as aware of it as he was, and they made sure he never had a chance to talk to the mine manager on his own, constantly floating around and distracting him away.

The Sheriff wasn't there at the beginning of the meeting, making his appearance half an hour later, with profuse apologies to his aunts. Herne had sharp hearing and he caught the words 'tomorrow noon' and wondered what that meant. He also puzzled over where Sheriff Daley had been. His shoulders were powdered with dust. The grey-orange sand that came from the mining operations back at Mount Morgoth.

After his arrival, Herne thought he detected an easing of tension. Though he didn't know why, he got the impression that Sheriff Daley had brought a secret message. Maybe they'd been checking on his credentials.

Maybe.

His room at *The Rich Nugget* was clean and quiet. There was something uncanny about Wild Rose City. Herne was almost tempted to go and visit the whore-house to see if that was as orderly as the rest of the town.

He'd tried asking the men in the saloon the same questions he'd asked at the meeting. About the robberies. Whether anyone had any clues.

Nobody did.

One old-timer suggested that it might be the Indians. 'Plenty of Sioux around here, Mister,' he said. 'Not so long since they took care of Yellow-Hair Custer.'

'Damned near ten years since the Little Big Horn,' Herne replied. 'Hasn't been any real trouble with the Sioux since then.'

'Anyway,' another man interrupted. 'Indians can't hardly process all that good ore.'

'True. So where is it being done? Can't be an operation you can readily hide.'

Jed had looked round the room in the sudden silence, waiting to see if anyone came up with any ideas. But nobody did. All at once everyone had got mighty interested in the contents of their glasses.

Something was wrong, but he just couldn't figure out what it was.

Next morning he got invited up to the big Sowren mansion for breakfast.

The dining-room was enormous. Long enough to exercise a horse in, with a table that would have seated fifty with comfort. As it was he found himself placed at one end, with Miss Lily at his right and Miss Eliza on his left. The meal gave him an indication of why the sisters were so totally different in build.

Eliza Sowten helped herself from only a couple of the soldierly row of polished silver chafing dishes that lined the side table. She had a single rasher of smoked Virginia ham and a tiny portion of omelette. Picking at it as though it was far too large a helping for her. Peering down her nose at it with bony distrust.

Lily went about as far as possible in the opposite direction.

Her plate was much larger than her sister's to begin with. Fork poised like a cavalry officer's sabre, she began with six slices of ham. A half dozen fried eggs, over easy. A mountain of hash browns with an equal helping of grits. Some smoked beans steaming on the side of the plate.

The smaller plate at her elbow was piled with corn bread, soaked in butter that threatened to run off the edge on the white cloth. Herne then noticed a third plate positioned directly in front of the fat old woman. With a mound of steaming buckwheat cakes on it, and a glass pitcher of warm molasses ready to pour.

The coffee pot would have held enough for half a regiment, and Lily didn't cut back any on the sugar. Putting in five heaped spoons, and pouring in a flood of thick cream.

Herne was more frugal, though anything would have seemed frugal by the side of such a gross exhibition of gluttony.

A single fresh trout with some hash browns was enough for him, though the fish was so large that its eyeless head drooped off one end of the platter and its tail off the other.

He washed it down with a couple of large cups of the excellent coffee, listening while the two sisters talked about the robberies. Trying to make out something that puzzled him. The Misses Sowren were obviously powerful. Indeed, there seemed no doubt at all that Wild Rose City was theirs to have and to hold. Nobody spat in the street without them knowing about it.

And their talk brimmed with their total confidence in their own prim rightness. Even their righteousness. They told him how awful these robberies had been, and how much harm it had done some of their local competitors. And how they had asked for the best bounty-hunter to be sent to them. All of that was fine.

So what was worrying them?

During the meal both of them kept shuffling in their seats. Lily straining her melon of a head on the wrestler's shoulders, as if she was listening for someone. Eliza darting her nose like a beak, seeking her prey.

Jed wondered who or what they were waiting for so impatiently.

Towards the end of the meal a maid came silently into the room and walked around to Eliza, leaning close and whispering something to her. Without replying, the younger of the sisters rose to her feet. Glaring at Herne who belatedly rose to his feet, his napkin falling to the floor as he did so, nearly spilling coffee all over the table.

'I have to go and sort out a small problem with the sheriff, Mister Herne. Perhaps you would be kind enough to wait here until I return. I'm sure that Lil will be happy to entertain you.'

The sisters stared at each other for a few moments, and Herne had the uncanny feeling that they were talking to each other in a way he couldn't understand. Then Lily nodded and rose to her feet, pressing down with her hands against the table to lever herself up.

'We have a pianoforte, Mister Herne. You may come and listen to my singing.'

If it was a request, it gave a fine impression of being a command. But it didn't make a lot of difference to Jed. There was something there and the longer he spent in the mansion, the more likely he was to ferret his way to the bottom of it.

Eliza stalked off, heels clicking on the polished wooden floor of the dining-room. Shortly after Herne heard the heavy front door slam shut. Lily was briefly busy again at her trough, face buried in a heap of treacly cakes, and he snatched a glance out of the long window. Just in time to see Sheriff Matthew Daley whipping up a pair of horses and driving a buckboard off down the steep hill, the braked rear wheels kicking a great cloud of dust behind him. Even through the sandy veil there was no mistaking the angular figure perched on the seat at his side.

Whatever Miss Eliza's small problem was, it seemed like it was rather more urgent than she'd made out.

Lily had insisted that Herne stood close enough to her to turn the pages of the music for her. Her fingers were so sticky from breaking her fast that he doubted she could have managed the chore for herself anyway. The ivory keys of the German piano were already stained and greasy from the attention of her fat little hands.

Her voice was low, insinuating itself into the ears of her unwilling listener. Herne had once visited the strange area close by the Yellowstone River, down in Wyoming, where natural hot springs forced water through the earth turning it into boiling mud. It was just that sinister sound that he recalled as he listened to Lily Sowren singing.

'*It begin to rain a little, de night was berry dark,*
De niggers dey got frightened and de dogs begin to bark,
De coon he scare de buzzard and de buzzard scare de coon,
And dey all keep on a-runnin' till tomorrow afternoon.'

Lily paused there and turned her face up towards Jed. Who noticed that in her exertions at the piano, she was sweating a great deal. The perspiration ravaging the heavy layers of make-up she wore. Opening up the crevices and furrows of old-age.

'Will you accompany me on the chorus, Mister Herne? Or might I call you Jedediah?'

'I think Mister Herne is better, Ma'am. Seein' as how I'm working for you. I don't care much for singing, if you'll pardon me, Miss Sowren.'

'Now that is a shame. Just care for killing, perhaps? You must tell me all about every single person you've killed, Mister Herne. *Every* one.'

It was an odd request, and Herne was disquieted to see a strange light in her eyes at the mention of killing.

'Not a fit topic for a lady, Miss Sowren.'

'Oh, fie on that! Just don't tell Liza, that's all. She doesn't approve. I just wondered if any of the men you had slaughtered were ... you must think me quite awful ... but I wondered if they had been in a state of nature.'

'How's that, Ma'am?'

'Unclad, Mister Herne.'

'Well, I guess some of the Indians might have been kind of short on clothes when they got sent to their hunting-ground in the sky.'

'You have butchered many Indians, Mister Herne? I am most impressed.'

'Paiutes in the snows of fifty-nine. I was just fifteen. Riding the Pony Express with Billy Cody. I figure over the years I've shot me plenty of Indians, Ma'am. Apaches, Sioux, Cheyenne.'

'That is wonderful.' She was sweating even more as they talked, the music forgotten for a moment.

'No, Ma'am.'

'No!'

'Begging your pardon, Miss Sowren, but I don't enjoy killing anyone. Well, I guess there's been one or two done me a personal wrong that I was glad to see dead. But the Indians fight us whites like a war. Like soldiers. If'n I hadn't killed some of them, they'd sure as ... they'd surely have killed me. It's not wonderful, Ma'am.'

'Oh. But there is talk that these noble savages have marvellous bodies. Developed more in some ways than those of white men.'

Her hand was resting on his arm, the fingers digging in convulsively and then relaxing, like a cat. Tightening and loosening and her voice had grown more hoarse.

'Can't say, Miss Sowren.' He was getting rapidly out of his depth in what he recognised were very murky waters indeed. 'Shouldn't we be gettin' on with this song? Your sister might be back real soon.'

'Oh, but this is so interesting! I have some books in my room that have pictures in them that you might find interesting. I have them sent privately through a close friend in Paris, France. They arrive under a plain cover with other items she sends me. She knows my tastes, you see, Mister Herne.'

The room was becoming stiflingly hot, the pressure of her hand tighter. Slipping down his arm.

Lower.

'I believe I hear Miss Eliza coming now,' he said, desperate to be away from this sick old lady. Masking God knows what unspeakable lusts behind the front of damask gentility and power.

'My goodness!' exclaimed Miss Lily, turning away from Jed so quickly she nearly knocked the pile of music from its stand on the piano, and it was only by a desperate grab that he was able to save it.

'I'm off to Charlestown, early in de mornin',
I'm off to Charlestown, with a little time to stay;
So give my respects to all of de friends,
I'm off to Charlestown before de break of day.'

*

She didn't seem at all put out that her sister didn't appear, carrying on singing with occasional accompaniment from Jed for more than an hour. The previous part of their conversation, bizarre though it had been, seemed to be quite forgotten by her. And Herne surely wasn't going to mention it. Just filing it away in his mind for future reference as part of the bewildering puzzle of Wild Rose City and the silver ore robberies.

Lily was still in full flow when Herne was relieved to see the reappearance of the buckboard rattling up Main Street, towards them. Miss Eliza was on her own and he wondered where the sheriff had gone. Even at a distance he could see that the old lady was smiling. A gash of red opened up under the prow of her nose.

'*Dear mother, sister, brother, all,*
One parting kiss to all goodbye;
Weep not, but clasp your hand in mine,
Pray let me like a soldier die!'

As she sang out the sad ballad, Herne noticed tears streaking Miss Lily Sowren's cheeks with the emotion of the song.

'*I've met the foe upon the field,*
Where many fiercely did defy,
I've fought for right – God bless our flag!
Dear mother, I've come home to die.'

Just as she was about to plunge into the last chorus, the door of the room swung silently open and in walked her sister, bringing a quick finale to the performance. Herne saw that the smile had disappeared and had been replaced by the usual formal, polite face. A mask. He wondered in passing what lay behind the mask.

'I trust I'm not interrupting anything, sister,' she said. 'It is such a scene of perfect bliss.'

'Indeed, sister, but Mister Herne and I have enjoyed a time of the most perfect bliss and happiness.'

'It is such a shame, Mister Herne,' said Eliza Sowren, 'that you must stay at the tavern.'

It took a moment for him to realise that she meant *The Rich Nugget*.

'Why is that, Miss Sowren?'

'Because you have given my sister so much pleasure with your company. It would have been quite wonderful if it had been possible for you to have moved in as our guest.'

'But I thought you've just arranged with ...' began Lily Sowren. Stopping dead in the middle of the sentence as she saw the look her younger sister turned on her. Herne was sideways on to it but the force of Eliza's anger blasted him as well, her eyes opening wide so that white showed all around the dark centre. Blazing with a rage that vanished as swiftly as it had appeared.

'You were thinking about the propriety of such an arrangement, were you not, sister?' she asked Lily, in a voice that dripped poisoned honey.

'Yes. Yes ... Of course ... I was thinking of precisely that, sister dear.'

'We have servants here and Mister Herne is somewhat different to the man we had expected, so I can see no harm in it.'

'How true, how true, Eliza,' said Lily, the colour returning to her cheeks.

'Well, Mister Herne? What do you think of the idea? Will you join us?'

He wondered just what was going on. The suggestion had clearly shaken Lily Sowren to the core of her ample being, but why? It seemed a sensible idea. There had to be something behind it.

'Don't see why not. I'm clean in thought, word and deed and I don't walk in my sleep or spit on the best carpets. Can I stable my horse up here as well?'

'Of course, Mister Herne.' A momentary hesitation from the distinguished-looking old lady. 'Would you like to go down now to the tavern and remove your possessions? I am sure our nephew Matthew will be in town to help you. He has a wagon you could borrow for your trunks.'

Herne laughed. Genuinely amused at how out of touch with reality the Misses Sowren were.

'Have I said something droll, Mister Herne?' snapped Eliza Sowren, mouth a narrow line of ice hanging beneath the cornice of her nose.

'No, Ma'am. Not exactly. But the idea of a man like me having a trunk, never mind a whole load of 'em! I travel light, Miss Sowren. Very light. One change of clothes. Slicker in case of rain. Ammunition for the pistol and the Sharps. And that's about all. Canteen of water and some jerky if'n I'm off on a journey. Nothing more.'

'What about soap?' asked Lily, standing up from the piano, lowering the lid quietly over the keys.

'Water in the streams, Miss Lily. I got me a razor I hone on my belt. Best I can do. Man riding for his life doesn't worry over much about smellin' of violets. More likely stinkin' of fear.'

'Mister Herne!' gasped Eliza.

'Sorry, Ma'am. But you asked me and I told you. If that offends you maybe you better choose your questions with a mite more care.'

This time it was Lily who gasped. Eyes so wide in the dumpling of a face that they seemed as if they were going to pop from their sockets.

'Nobody speaks to my sister like that, Herne.'

'I do. You don't like it then I can go and report back and someone else'll come along.'

With a tremendous effort Eliza Sowren regained her self-control. Breathing hard and speaking through tight lips to him.

'Very well, Mister Herne. Let us accept that you are a rough diamond, unlike most of the decent people here in Wild Rose City.'

'Decent folks don't kill, Miss Sowren. They just pay men like me to do it for 'em so they can keep their hands clean and their consciences whiter than white.'

He was deliberately pushing at the elderly woman. Trying to rile her into being indiscreet. Into letting slip some clue to help him understand what was happening.

But she was clever. Too wise to be angered by his goading.

'I think we must agree to differ somewhat on that, Mister Herne. But our offer still stands. Will you join us here until this business is sorted out?'

'Sure. Doesn't affect my pay?'

'No. My sister and I will make sure that you receive everything that you have earned.'

As he walked down the hill towards the saloon to collect his things, Herne reflected that what Eliza had just said could have been either a promise.

Or a threat.

Wild Rose seemed virtually deserted.

It was close to noon and even the sheriff's office was locked up. The battered rocker deserted outside the barred door. The saloon was empty, except for a young boy, still in his teens, at the far end of the bar.

He was drinking a glass of beer, standing sideways on

to the door. Jed noticed him immediately, registering several other facts at the same time.

First off was the gun.

A forty-five like Jed's own. Worn very low on the right hip. The retaining thong slipped clear of the hammer ready for a fast draw. The rig tied to the thigh. Lower than Herne would have thought advisable. It meant the kid would have to reach that couple of inches further than necessary. When two closely matched shootists met, a couple of inches meant the difference between the free drinks and the free burial.

The other thing that set the short hairs at the nape of Jed's neck prickling was that the saloon was totally empty. Not even the bar-keep was there. Just Herne.

And the kid.

He half-turned and reached down to his own hip, flicking off the narrow cord that held his pistol in its holster. Just in case it was needed.

'You Herne?'

The voice was confident. Cocky. The sort of voice that he'd heard a thousand times before. In saloons and brothels and streets all the way from the Rio Grande to the Canadian border.

'Yeah.'

'Herne the Hunter?'

'Some say so.'

The boy was turned to face him, already slipping into a half-crouch. The beginnings of the gunfighter's classic stance. Presenting the left side of your body to your enemy, giving him a smaller target.

'You're a hell of an old man for such a big name. Looks likely you're livin' on a few things years back. Maybe you once shot a marshal in the back, and men've been feared of you since. What do you say to that?'

Herne felt tired. Scenting death on the young boy.

Knowing that this one was going to have to be played all the way through to the end.

Wondering what had brought a punk killer like this into *The Rich Nugget* at the same time as himself. Considering whether to begin to add two and two.

His arithmetic interrupted by the boy's voice. Harsh and amused by something he thought was going to be easy.

'I'm goin' out, old man. Less'n you're a dirty yellow bastard, you'll face me. What do you say?'

Herne shook his head slowly, speaking low. 'I say that next time I want some shit I'll just need to squeeze your head.'

CHAPTER FOUR

For a moment Herne had thought the boy was going to lose his self-control and make a play against him right there in the saloon. It didn't matter much to Jed if he had. An angry gun-fighter was a bad gun-fighter, and it never hurt to edge the odds your way.

There'd been a lot of times that Jed had faced men ready to draw against him, and he was still alive. Most all of them were dead.

But that didn't make him any less careful. He'd seen too many friends get to buy the farm from being careless.

And he knew well enough what a waste of time it was to try the soft answer. Nine times out of ten you still had to fight, and all you did was give the other man confidence. It just came down to being firstest with the mostest.

'You son of a...'

'Talk's cheap son. Let's go out in the street where the action is. See what price you want to pay.'

They faced each other, Herne wondering whether the boy would try it there and then. Knowing that he'd take him out. Seeing the glimmer of uncertainty as he realised that Herne looked very big and very mean. And that Herne didn't seem worried by the challenge. Or frightened by it.

'All right, old man. You go first.'

'Let you shoot me in the back? I'm full of that kind of trick, son. Come on over and we walk out slow and easy. Together.'

The sun was almost directly overhead as they stepped out of the cool of the saloon onto the boardwalk along the street. The kid edgy and tense. Herne calm and relaxed.

On the outside he was calm and relaxed.

Inside he was tightened up to a hair-trigger readiness. Looking around for the sign of movement or the glitter of light off a gun that would mean he was being set up by the kid for friends in the street.

Suddenly the town was full of people.

Every window had its crowd of faces; every door was partly open with a person in the shadows. Just for a terrifying moment Jed thought they were all out to get him and he almost began the draw, knowing it was over but determining to go down blasting.

Then he realised that they were just spectators. Out to watch the killing as if they were going to a picnic or a barn-raising.

So they'd known.

Known the young boy was in there, and knowing what was going to happen.

Wild Rose City, so pretty and clean on the outside, was beginning to smell like a week dead horse when you got closer.

'I'll walk that way, son,' said Herne, starting to pace off to the left, down the hill.

'You'll get the sun in my eyes, damn you!' snarled the kid.

'Sun's clean overhead,' replied Jed, calmly. 'But if'n you want the lower end, you take it. No concern to me.'

'Hell! You're tryin' to fuckin' trick me, you stinkin' old bastard.'

'You think what you want, boy. I'm givin' you the choice.' He kept his voice loud so that everyone watching would hear. Would know that he wasn't trying to railroad the young man into the fight. When you got to be a top shootist, then you had to take a lot of care. Otherwise you won the fight and still ended up dead. Choking out your life on the end of a vigilante rope.

'You go down the hill, old-timer,' shouted the boy, starting to walk, stiff-legged away from Jed.

Who turned and walked a dozen paces down. That was what he'd wanted all along. It was easier to aim up a hill rather than down. If you missed your chest shot you had a good chance of at least taking the man in the legs. Miss when you were shooting down a hill, and the odds were that you'd miss high and the bullet would go whining harmlessly by.

There was the rattling of a wagon in the small alley that ran along the back of Main Street, and Herne saw a cloud of dust drifting across the rear of the buildings. Wondering who was in such a hurry to come and see the fight. Having a sneaking suspicion of the answer to his own question. Seeing the answer when the Misses Sowren appeared around the corner of the bank, joining the manager, their oldest son, Joab, by the front door. Watching eagerly.

Two and two started to add up to four.

The kid was around eighteen. Maybe nineteen. He had grown a drooping moustache to try and make himself look older, and his hair hung across his narrow shoulders. He was wearing a light coloured jacket and a blue shirt, open almost to his stomach.

His face was thin and foxy, eyes slitted in a pale face. Herne didn't recognise him as a top gun, though shootists were always springing up and getting themselves a reputation for a few months in any town along the border or in the north where the mines were. Then the day came along when they met someone that inch faster or luckier, and their reputation didn't shield them from lead.

'Right Mister Herne. You ready now, you spit-suckin' old bastard?'

'Ready as I'll ever be, boy,' replied Herne, flexing his shoulders, feeling the coat across his back. Moving the fingers of his right hand to ease away any stiffness.

'Don't fuckin' call me "boy", you son of a damned bitch, Herne. Don't you want to know my name?'

'Never concerned myself with the name of a man I'm goin' to kill, son. Let's get to it.'

The crowd was edging out into the open. The saloon was suddenly filled with folks, including Marcus Daley, a white towel across his arm. Herne wondered which of the Sowren's brood ran the morticians' parlour.

The dry goods store was at his back, the clerk, Hempstead, peering out from the front window, behind a display of cracker biscuits. The ladies gathered by the bank.

The sheriff hadn't put in an appearance yet. That surprised Herne.

The two men faced each other. One young, coiled like a spring. The other grizzled and relaxed. Hands hanging loose at his side.

The shot made everyone jump. Booming out from the side of Main Street.

Herne began to turn, seeing the burst of powder smoke, even before he'd registered the crack of the shot. Then easing off again as he saw it was Sheriff Daley, putting in a belated word for law and order in the town.

'You men better back off there,' he shouted, holding his smoking pistol in his hand. It wasn't much of a threat from better than fifty yards off but Herne watched him cautiously, trying to figure out the rules that this game was being played under. Careful not to make any sort of move that could be interpreted as menacing the lawman.

'Leave us be, Sheriff,' called the boy, his voice cracking with the tension, wobbling from foot to foot as if he was about to dive for cover.

'I said back off. Can't kill around here.'

'Fair fight, Sheriff Daley,' shouted someone from the crowd by the livery stables.

A voice that Herne would have sworn came from Gawain Sowren, Eliza's youngest son.

'Don't allow no fightin', in this town. Not fair fights and not unfair ones.'

'Stand back, Sheriff!' shouted the kid. 'Me and this old man got us some shootin' to do.'

'Now you both . . .'

'Matt. Leave them be.'

The sheriff turned round as though someone had just nudged him with a branding-iron, staring across at where his aunt stood with her sister.

'But we said . . .'

'Let it be, Matthew,' replied Eliza Sowren. 'They wish to have a fair fight, then let them. I can see no harm in it. Unless Mister Herne wishes to back down from it.'

Jed didn't. But it was interesting that she should suggest it. Almost as if she was able to control the kid and the way he acted. Like she controlled her own kin.

Almost.

'Well, I don't rightly . . .'

'I do, Matthew. Do as I tell you and let them get on with it. I'm sure that Mister Herne will uphold the right for Wild Rose City against young . . . this boy.'

For a moment it was as though she knew the kid's name and then remembered she didn't. But that didn't worry Herne right at that moment. His eyes were locked with those of the young boy in the light jacket. Wondering if he would be one of those that stood still or one that powered himself off to the side as he opened fire.

'Very well,' shouted the sheriff, trying to salvage a remnant of his lost pride from the situation. 'You fight fair now. And I figure maybe it's better if'n I give you the signal to . . .'

'Sheriff,' shouted the boy, coming close to winning a touch of respect from Herne. 'You and men like you don't understand what's going down here between me and this old man. Just leave it alone or . . .'

The threat dangled in the dirt of the street, lying there among the short black shadows of the two men. The old and the young.

Jed watched Daley out of the corner of his eye, seeing him looking in his turn to his aunts, standing close together. One lean and tall, the other round and short.

'All right. But it'd better be fair. Man tries to draw unfair and I'll gun him down in the dirt, so help me, God.'

'Matthew,' warned Eliza Sowren, thin-lipped at the blasphemy.

The buzz of conversation in the crowd died slowly down, leaving the two of them facing each other, around twenty paces apart. Waiting.

'Make your play, old man.'

Herne shook his head. 'Never drawn first on a man or a boy in my life, son. You can get started and I'll kind of catch you up.'

It wasn't true. There had been times when Jed had shot first. Times even when he'd shot men in the back. If it was your life there on the line, and the cards were stacked against you, then there was no point in giving it up.

But faced with a kid, and a kid whose holster was slung way too low, Herne figured he could afford to be that bit generous. It wasn't as though as he was facing Billy Bonny. He had once. Years back. Hell, the Kid was dead and buried these four years. He'd been about the fastest had Billy. Runty son of a bitch. Laughed when he ate. Laughed when he made love. Laughed when he stole. Laughed when he killed men. Jed had always wondered whether Billy had laughed when Pat gunned him down at Pete Maxwell's.

Top shootists hardly ever faced each other like this in a high noon pistol duel. They always knew how fast they were. And how tiny was the margin between the best and the second. So small that nobody could ever swear that it even existed.

So there wasn't any point. Maybe you'd get the first bullet off and kill the other. But it was a better than even wager he'd have had enough time to squeeze his own trigger and you could be dead or critically wounded at the same time.

It wasn't worth it.

'Come on, Herne!'

It was a beautiful day. The fresh spring air of the Dakotas and the foaming waters of the river as a backdrop to the town. The hills all around it. The only cloud against the blue sky to the west where the Mount Morgoth refinery belched out filthy smoke.

'Draw, damn you!'

'Told you before, sonny. You wanted me out here so you get on with it. Or take out your gun and throw it down. Walk away and you stay alive, son.'

'Draw!!'

'No.'

'Bastard!!!'

The kid screamed at the top of his voice, hand slapping

down, body ducking and beginning to twist, knees bending. Herne reacting like a prairie rattler. Hand blurring for the butt of the forty-five. So much faster than the boy.

Three fingers around the polished wood, drawing the gun easily from the greased leather. Thumb pulling back on the hammer, triple-clicking into place. Index finger snug and tight around the thin trigger of the pistol.

All happening by habit. His brain not even aware that it was going on. An instinctive movement, all worked in with the drawing and levelling of the gun. The movement of the body, the left arm balancing the right.

The kid wasn't that bad. Herne had killed plenty slower. Not bad for a small town hidden away in the middle of the Black Hills. But he wouldn't have lasted an hour in Tucson or Tombstone against real gunmen.

In the background, just before he squeezed the trigger, Herne was aware of a sound he'd heard a lot of times before. The gasp of a crowd seeing a man draw a gun faster than any of them could have believed possible. Herne wasn't just good. Not just fast.

He was about the best.

Slightly higher than him, standing up the slope of the street, the kid took the first bullet in the pit of the stomach. With his pistol still not clear of the holster. The forty-five slug kicking him a couple of steps back, the gun dropping from his fingers. Both hands reaching for the wound as if he couldn't believe what was happening. Eyes staring wide, jaw gaping in shock.

It would probably have been enough. Any bullet that got itself buried deep in your stomach in eighteen eighty-five would generally kill you.

Quick or slow. Often slow. And painful.

Jed wasn't in the waiting mood.

'One to kill them. Two to set your mind easy.' That was

what someone had once said to him. Couldn't recall the name. Might have been that ex-officer. Caleb something. Thorn. Or maybe it was the man that folks just called Crow. No other name. Probably Crow. Meanest and coldest son of a bitch Jedediah Herne had ever met. Cavalry man.

The second bullet took the young boy's feet the last steps along the road to the shrine of death.

The kid was fighting to straighten up from the bullet in the stomach when the second slug hit him. Ripping his throat apart, snapping splinters of bone from the top of his spine, and bursting on through the back of his neck in a gout of bright arterial blood.

He dropped to his knees, coughing, hands resting in the dirt. Gripping the small stones of the street so hard that Herne could actually hear the boy's nails snapping and tearing backwards as the pain beat him down.

Blood pattered in the sand, loud in the quietness, clearly audible even above the noise of the Clearwater River and a sigh from the crowd. The ragged breathing of the dying boy, bubbling through the frothing blood from his lungs, was the only other sound. Herne watched him, the smoking pistol still in his fist, a cartridge ready under the cocked hammer.

'Herne ...' panted the kid, raising his head with an agonising effort.

'What is it, son?' asked the older man, stepping a few paces nearer.

'Herne ... They said ... to me ...' A coughing fit interrupted him and he slid forwards on his face, the blood flowing more slowly from the wounds at front and back of his neck. Barely trickling from the other wound in his stomach.

Jed took another couple of steps, trying to hear what the kid was saying. Watching him carefully in case he was going to try a last trick. The fallen pistol was only inches from the boy's clawing fingers.

'Who told you, son?' he asked.

'They ...'

'They?'

The face turned up to him, slobbered with blood, bubbles smeared across his mouth. Spotting the blue shirt and dappling the white jacket. The boy's eyes were veiling over as he became preoccupied with the mystery of his own dying.

'The ...'

The bullet smashed into the back of his skull, bouncing his face in the dirt. Herne spun around at the shot, gun seeking out who'd fired it. Seeing the pistol in the chubby hand of Sheriff Matthew Daley. Who waved it apologetically at him before holstering it.

'Sorry, Mister Herne. Thought I saw him going for his gun.'

Jed looked down, seeing that the boy's hand *was* close to the butt of the pistol, the fingers now relaxing in death. Looking up again into the frank, open face of the ageing lawman.

'That's the case then I got to thank you. And I got to go lookin' for someone else owes you a debt of thanks.'

'Who?'

'Persons the kid was goin' to name before you blasted the words off his lips.'

'What are you sayin' Herne?' asked Daley, fingers hooked belligerently in his wide belt.

'I'm sayin' nothing, Sheriff. And neither is he.'

CHAPTER FIVE

Four days drifted by and not a great deal happened in Wild Rose City.

Jed Herne moved his saddle-bags and Sharps rifle into the Sowren mansion, and his horse into the luxurious stable at the back of the sprawling house, on the side overlooking the cemetery.

The weather changed for the worse.

It had been perfect spring days, when Jed reached the town. The Dakota Territory looking at its best in the warm greening. Now the skies had darkened, the whole region buried under a leaden pall. Old-timers said the rains were coming, but each day stayed dry. The wind rose, kicking up dust across the river, whipping up the clouds from north to south. And it became colder.

It was a cold day when they buried the kid that Herne had gunned down. Nobody went. Jed didn't see much point and it seemed that there wasn't anyone else in the whole of Wild Rose that knew him. Which was strange. Considering the reception Jed had received from Sheriff Daley when he thought he was a saddle tramp. Yet there was this kid, a born killer from his looks, drinking alone and in style in the saloon. The town was an enigma shrouded in mystery.

On the kid's grave they stuck a wooden marker. It didn't say much. Wasn't much to say. The day and the month and the year. And the words: 'A boy of about eighteen not so fast as he figured'.

It was a fair enough epitaph.

There wasn't a whole lot Jed could do. He'd been hired to try and prevent any shipments from Mount Morgoth being stolen. Since there wasn't a shipment due for a couple of weeks, he considered going and trying to gain some information from other mines in the area. But this was checked by Eliza Sowren.

'We are having an excellent year at our mine, Mister Herne. And it is our mine and ours alone that you have been hired to protect. Let the other owners look to their own precautions. We all know each other around here. Indeed, some of my family have on occasions ridden out to try and help other shipments get through. But this is a different matter. You are not family, Mister Herne.'

'Indeed not, sister,' Lily had said, appearing suddenly in the room from upstairs. Herne had noticed that the massively overweight sister disappeared to her room most afternoons for a rest. Yet he sometimes heard the noise of movement and once, as he passed by, he was sure he could hear her groaning in the room. If it hadn't been locked he might have risked a look in from simple curiosity, even though it was none of his business.

'It is none of your business, Mister Herne,' Eliza had continued. 'Kindly remain in Wild Rose City or at the mine. Sheriff Daley or one of the other boys will accompany you if you travel to Mount Morgoth. It is a perilous region with many abandoned shafts and pits there. We would not wish anything to happen to you.'

'Indeed not, sister,' added Lily.

'Indeed not, ladies,' Herne had felt bound to say, bowing to both of them.

It was a strange job.

He decided that he must get to the mine, and try and have a word with the nervous Mister Zimmerman. Jed wished he could have shaken off his tail, but whenever he wanted to leave the immediate limits of Wild Rose, there was always someone there. Generally the sheriff. Sometimes the fat mayor, Julius. Once it was the solemn Joab, riding a sedate chestnut mare.

But he was never alone.

Once he'd tried to slip casually away, but there was Matthew Daley. Sitting on his horse, chewing on a piece of tobacco, spitting a brown stream in the dirt in front of Herne's stallion. Grinning at him.

If he was ever going to get to the bottom of the layers of mystery that covered the problem, Jed knew that he'd have to step easy and clever.

So he simply called in at the office of the lawman and said he wanted to go up to the mine and would Matthew come along.

They rode together, mainly in silence, through the dull morning, along the winding trail to the mine.

'Looks like there's some dirty weather on the way, Jedediah,' said Daley.

'Looks that way. The Clearwater's high, considering the warm spell. That melt water?'

'Yeah. If'n we get rain now like the sky looks, it could burst over. Happened before. Guess it'll happen again. Who do you want to see up there?'

'Manager. Just look around.'

'Sure. Bob Zimmerman's a funny guy. Kind of nervy. Know what I mean?'

'Can't say I do.'

'Kind of sees things aren't there.'

'Ghosts?'

Daley reined in his horse, turning to stare at Herne. 'You know I don't mean that.'

Since the efficient way Jed had disposed of the kid, the sheriff had been more respectful towards him. Taking care with him.

'Then what do you mean, Sheriff?'

'I mean you shouldn't listen too careful to some of the things he says.'

'Come on, Daley. Either crap or get the Hell off the pot. What do you *mean*?'

'I mean Zimmerman's a liar. Dreamer. He got wounded back in the war.'

'So did lots of guys. I did.'

'Sure I know that. Lots of innocent people got hurt in it.'

For a moment Herne's mind flashed back to the dreadful massacre at Lawrence, Kansas. When he and the albino, Whitey Coburn, rode with Quantrill and his infamous Raiders. Plenty of innocent people killed amid the flames and slaughter of that doomed town.*

'So what's special about Zimmerman?'

'Morphine.'

'Got its hooks in him?'

Daley nodded. 'Yeah. They gave him that heroin stuff to get him off the morphine. Then that caught him. They call it . . .'

'The "Army Disease",' interrupted Herne. 'I know that. And the manager's caught it?'

* The story of the Lawrence raid can be read in Herne 9: 'Massacre', also available from Corgi Books.

'So they say. Reckons he's clear of it now. But he's kind of strange. I'll stick around while you talk to him, if'n you don't mind.'

'I don't mind at all, Sheriff,' replied Herne, deciding there and then to do everything in his power to get to talk to the mysterious Zimmerman alone.

The manager of the Mount Morgoth mine looked even more pale and nervous than when Herne had seen him first nearly a week ago. His curly hair was straggled and uncombed, strands of it stuck to his high forehead. Sweat trickled down the side of his nose as he greeted them, even though the day was quite cool. His eyes flicked from man to man, yet never quite looking at either of them. And he licked his lips a lot.

Jed had seen people infected by a need for morphine, and for the newer drug, heroin, before and he thought he recognised some of the symptoms. The haggard face and sunken eyes. The way Zimmerman's hands constantly played with each other, the fingers tangling and knotting.

'Good to see you, gentlemen,' he said. 'Anything special I can do for you?'

'Herne wants a look around. That's all. I came with him because a mine and smelting plant can be kind of dangerous, can't they, Bob?'

'Yes. Yes, Sheriff, they can.'

'And we don't want any foolish mistakes or accidents, do we?'

Zimmerman attempted a laugh that didn't work. And a smile to go with it that never even made it as far as his lips.

'Sure don't. Guess the Misses Sowren wouldn't take to that, Sheriff.'

'Guess not. Let's get to it, shall we?'

'Sure thing. Anything Mister Herne specially wants to see?' Glancing sideways at Jed.

'Yeah.'

'What?'

'Everything, Mister Zimmerman. I'd like to see just about everything.'

It was like a lot of other mines in other towns. There didn't seem anything special about it. The refinery was working flat-out, even though there seemed rather less activity on the actual ore-mining side of the operation.

Jed picked his moment to play a hunch. Waiting until they were in the refinery, amid the noise and bustle and heat and stink. Choosing an opportunity when some trucks were being wheeled past along rusted rails. Their axles squeaking and grinding. Sheriff Daley was temporarily cut off from Zimmerman and Herne.

'Miss Sowren said the mine was well down on last year, Mister Zimmerman,' he said.

If he'd whispered that he was really Pope Leo XIII visiting America in disguise he would hardly have got a better reaction.

'What?' said the manager. But the word somehow got lost between his brain and his mouth and no sound actually came out. He tried again. 'She said that?'

'Yes. Said the mine wasn't doing all that well, this year.'

'But I thought that Miss Eliza and Miss Lily had promised . . .'

Daley spotted the private moment and came quickly over to them, cursing as he dodged the line of clattering trucks.

'Promised what, Zimmerman?'

Herne got in before the stammering manager could reply.

'I was saying that Miss Eliza had said what a great year Mount Morgoth was having. Mister Zimmerman was telling me that the ladies had promised not to mention it here in case the men wanted more money and used it as an excuse.'

It was a clever lie. Hardly on the spur of the moment as Herne was ready for the Sheriff to try and catch him out. But it worked.

'That so, Mister Zimmerman?'

'What?'

'That true, what Mister Herne here said? Is it right?'

'Yes. Of course, Sheriff. What Mister Herne said is quite correct. Absolutely correct in every single detail. Correct.'

Herne was glad that Daley was moving, not noticing the way that the manager's hands were shaking. Zimmerman excused himself for a few minutes shortly after that, mumbling something about a little dog. Herne didn't catch what, but it seemed to be an excuse to get away and regain the nervous state that passed, in his case, for composure.

When he reappeared he did look better and Jed wondered whether he had given himself an injection of the drug that Daley claimed possessed him.

At the end of the tour all three men walked to the top of the hill that dominated the area, looking back towards Wild Rose City. Herne noticed that the Sowren's great mansion commanded a view over an amazing expanse of land. From their upper windows the sisters were able to look out not only over their own little kingdom of the town, but also clean across the knife-edged canyons to the mine and smelting plant.

'Is there anything else you wish to see, Mister Herne?' asked the little man, now keeping his hands firmly in the pockets of his grey jacket. Perhaps to hide his nerves from Daley.

'I don't think so, thanks, Mister Zimmerman. You've shown me all there is, I guess.'

'Oh, no. Given a better opportunity I believe I could show you much, much more.'

The sheriff was gazing homewards, taking little notice of the social requirements of their leaving, and he didn't seem to hear the emphasis that Zimmerman gave to his last words. Nor did he see the glance that the manager gave Herne. A look of entreaty that bordered on desperation.

'Good day to you, sir,' said Herne, shaking hands with Zimmerman. Blinking as he felt something pressed in his fingers by the manager. But giving no other sign of his surprise.

'Good day, Mister Herne. I hope we shall meet again.'

'I hope so. Coming Sheriff?'

'Sure,' grunted Daley. 'So long, Zimmerman. You take care now, you hear?'

'Of course, Sheriff. So long.'

As they walked away Jed looked back once and saw the slight figure standing alone on the side of the tip of waste ore. Looking somehow isolated – and vulnerable.

On the short ride back to Wild Rose, Herne reassured Daley that he thought Zimmerman a nervous old woman. The sheriff reined in and glanced across at him with a sly grin on his beefy face.

'Wouldn't use an expression like that around town if'n I was you, Herne.'

'Like what?'

'Nervous old woman. My aunts might be old women but you better not make the mistake of thinkin' they're nervous. They ain't.'

Herne didn't reply. Waiting until he was alone in the

stable at the mansion at the top of the hill to reach in his own pocket and pull out the note that Zimmerman had pushed in his hand as he left the Mount Morgoth mine. It was scrawled in pencil and showed the panic of the manager in its hasty composition.

'*You know truth silver roberys all around meet sunup tomorow where river bends back of Monroe place.*' It wasn't signed.

It didn't need to be.

CHAPTER SIX

The Clearwater had risen better than two feet during the night.

It was a sure sign that rain had been falling heavily up in the high country of the Dakotas, adding to the burden of the melt run-off.

Herne stood under a small grove of cottonwoods, scarcely visible in the pearly light of early morning, waiting to see if Zimmerman would keep his nerve long enough to show up for their meeting.

It had been easy to get out of the Sowren mansion without being observed. The servants who rose before dawn had their quarters at the back of the house, and nobody saw Jed as he crept silently out. The sky was lightening towards the east, with the first signs of the false dawn, but it would be a full hour or more before it became properly light. By then he hoped that his business would be finished and he could be safely back in the high feather-bed with the polished brass frame.

The sky was completely clouded over and a thin mist hung across the lower end of the valley, its tendrils reaching half-way up Main Street, about to the dry goods store. But stopping short of the Sowren house as if it didn't dare to come any closer without incurring the wrath of the redoubtable ladies sleeping within.

Herne bent down and picked up a handful of tiny pebbles, flicking them absently into the surging waters of the river.

Hunching his shoulders protectively against the cold and damp. There was so much water carried in the air that it didn't make a lot of difference whether it was actually raining or not. The effect was the same. For a moment he wished he'd brought out his oilskin, but it was an impossible garment to wear or carry quietly, with its crackling folds, and he decided he'd made the right decision. It wouldn't be a good thing if Miss Eliza or Miss Lily were to see him meeting secretly with their mine manager. Though what Zimmerman had to tell him was beyond Herne's guesswork. But it had to be worth hearing.

He glanced back up the hill and wondered whether it would be possible for anyone in the house to see him. Deciding that they couldn't. It was a good quarter mile and the visibility was very poor.

There was the sound of stones shifting underfoot, further down the valley, towards the mine. Herne checked automatically that the leather cord was free of the top of the Colt's hammer. Wild Rose City was such a peculiar place that it was a fool who didn't take precautions. And out West a fool didn't get to live very long.

'Mister Herne,' hissed a voice. High and thin and trembling, like the summer wind through pine trees.

Jed stood still and waited. Wanting to see whether Zimmerman had come alone or whether he was just the judas goat in a trap. There was a silence and then he caught the noise of feet coming closer, slipping on the pebbles, somewhere to the left, on the same side of the river as Herne. Easing towards him.

'Mister Herne. Are you there?'

He still waited, not wanting to reveal where he was, deep in a pool of shadow. Able to see without being seen.

'It's me. Bob Zimmerman. Are you there? Oh, Jesus Christ!'

It was almost a cry of despair, so rending in the early morning that Jed immediately believed the manager's honesty. Nobody could act terror that well. The little man from Hibbing was so frightened that you could damned nearly smell it.

'I'm here. And keep your voice quiet, less'n you want the whole damned town to know we're meeting here like this!'

'Where are you?'

'Under the trees.'

'Where?'

'Here.'

'Oh. I think I see you. I'm just ... Ooooh ... My God! I nearly fell into the river, Mister Herne.'

With the Clearwater running as high as it was Herne had no doubts that Zimmerman would inevitably have been swept away to his death.

One thing was certain.

Though he was a good swimmer, Jed wouldn't have gone into the icy waters after him.

The mist wavered as a breath of wind came up from the north, and Herne was at last able to see the manager of the Mount Morgoth mine. Staggering slightly as he fought for his footing on the wet pebbles. He was wearing a dark suit and ankle boots. An outfit better suited to Boston than a muddy trail in the Black Hills. Jed noticed that Zimmerman had obviously fallen several times on his stumbling journey through the darkness and his clothes were smeared with dirt, black patches of wetness showing in the pale light.

'Thank God you've come, Mister Herne,' he panted, reaching out to shake Jed by the hand. As he took it, Herne felt the chill from his fingers. Fingers that were quivering with fear.

'What have you got to tell me, Zimmerman? About the robberies?'

'I've worked at Mount Morgoth for several years now, since I first came to Dakota Territory. Before that I had been . . .'

'Christ, Zimmerman,' said Herne disgustedly. 'I didn't come out here in this lousy weather just to listen to the story of your life!'

'I'm sorry. Oh, God, but I'm so sorry, Mister Herne.' For a moment Jed thought the manager was going to break down and start weeping. The damp had plastered his thin curly hair across his forehead and there was a streak of dark mud under one cheekbone. The eyes were sunken in and he coughed nervously, putting his hand to his mouth. Jed saw that even since the previous day the man's condition had worsened. He was blinking constantly.

'Come on. Get a damned grip on yourself. Tell me what you have to say and we can both go.'

'Yes. You're right, of course. It's just that I so wanted . . .'

'Zimmerman,' warned Herne.

'Yes. It's about the robberies. I . . . I know something about them.'

'What?'

'I know who's doing them, Mister Herne.'

'Who?'

'I'm sorry. I can't tell you.'

There was a short silence between them. Jed considered drawing the pistol and bending it across Zimmerman's face. There wasn't a shred of doubt in his mind that the manager really did know.

'What the Hell is that supposed to mean?' he snarled.

'It's just that . . .'

'Just fuckin' nothing, Zimmerman, you gutless son of a bitch!!'

There was no need to fake his annoyance. Herne was bitterly angry with the little curly-headed man for getting him out there in such a dangerous way, then losing his nerve.

'I can't tell you.'

'Why not?'

'They'll kill me. They'll know who . . . who told on them, and they'll kill me.'

Reassurance was useless and Jed recognised that immediately. What the true story was might be something he could only guess at. And he was beginning to guess at it.

'All right. Calm down.' Despite his rage he forced himself to pat Zimmerman on the shoulder, wanting nothing more than to take the honed bayonet from its sheath in his right boot and cut the manager here and there until he blurted out what he knew. But it wasn't the time or the place for that. It was time for the carrot rather than the stick.

'I'm sorry, Mister Herne. Truly I'm . . .' and to his embarrassment the manager of Mount Morgoth began to weep in his arms, his slight body racked with juddering sobs.

'Come on. There must be some help that you can give me without betraying . . . anyone.' The pause was where Herne nearly took a chance and voiced his suspicions, holding back from it because he was worried what the effect might be on Zimmerman.

'Help?'

'Damn it, man, that's what we're both down here for, isn't it?'

'Yes.' Hesitantly.

'Then come on. It'll soon be full light and they'll be able to see us from every damned house in Wild Rose City. And that is going to make folks mighty suspicious, Mister Zimmerman.'

'I can tell you one thing.'

'What?'

'The next robbery.'

'Yeah? Go on.'

'I know when.'

'Tell me.'

'And where.'

'But not who?'

'No.'

'Sure?'

'I'm positive. Please don't ask me that, Mister Herne. I beg you.'

He was gradually regaining his control, standing away from Jed, wiping his nose with a white square of linen that he unfolded from a pocket of his vest. Blowing noisily and then sniffing, flicking away the remains of a tear from his cheek.

'Better now, Zimmerman?'

'Yes.'

'So, tell me.'

'Tomorrow.'

'Tomorrow!'

'Yeah.'

'Jesus, Zimmerman! You surely don't give a lot of warning, do you?'

'It's taken all my courage, Mister Herne, even to tell you this much.'

'I need more.'

'It's from Old Number One Mine, again. They've already hit it once.'

'Where?'

'Close by. About eleven miles north and west of town there's a narrow canyon, with several spur canyons opening off it. Most of them are boxed, but there are some with trails through wide enough for a man on a horse leading pack mules.'

'What time tomorrow?'

Zimmerman looked at the mud staining his boots and

shuffled his feet nervously. Herne stared at him in disgust, unable to understand how fear could so reduce a person's will. Once you let fright rule you, then it ruled for ever. All you had to do was stand up to it. The worst that could happen to a man was death. Herne stopped being afraid of dying a very long time ago.

'I asked you what time tomorrow the robbery's goin' to be?'

'Later on. Probably close to evening. They leave the mine in the morning, and they should be passing through here on their way to Jansonville by nightfall.'

'That's all you're goin' to tell me?'

'I . . . I guess so, Mister Herne. I think I ought to be gettin' back now, before I'm missed. There's eyes everywhere watchin' around Wild Rose.'

All the time Herne's suspicions were becoming stronger and stronger.

Unbelievable though they seemed to him, the trail of clues seemed to be pointing in only one possible direction.

'Guess you better go. Me too. Wouldn't do for the ladies to catch me sneakin' out like this.' A thought struck him. 'But I surely am kind of doin' the job they hired me for. Trackin' down these killers who've been stealin' silver ore all over the damned Dakotas.'

'Sure is,' stammered the manager, staring all around him as the light grew into a great halo in the east, making it possible to see further down and up the valley. Somehow the swelling brightness seemed to make the turbulent river sound quieter.

'How many men goin' to be there tomorrow evening, Zimmerman? Seems I'm goin' to have to try it all on my own, so you owe me that much.'

'I'm not sure.'

'God damn it! Be sure!' hissed Herne, grabbing him

by the collar and lifting him clear off the ground in one hand, his legs jerking and kicking helplessly. Zimmerman's face began to turn purple, his tongue protruding. His eyes seemed to swell from their sockets.

'Please . . .' he gasped.

'Please, nothin',' spat Jed. 'I don't know what you're frightened of, Mister, but whatever it is you better believe I can top it.'

He dropped him contemptuously to the wet stones, watching him sprawl on his side, rolling nearly into the Clearwater, panting for breath, running his shaking fingers around the inside of his collar.

'Now you tell me how many. I'm not askin' you who's behind it. I see that one's too much for you. But you must tell me how many.'

'They might see us here,' panted Zimmerman, scrambling painfully to his hands and knees, not looking at Herne.

'To see us here they'd need to be up damned high with a spyglass, and I don't see no signs of that happening. So come on.'

'Two or three this time. Doubt there's goin' to be more, Mister Herne. Truly. They know how the ore is being carried. How many guards.'

'How do they know that?'

But Zimmerman remained stubbornly silent.

'Late evening. What's the name of the canyon where it's to happen?'

'Drowned Squaw Canyon. Can't miss it. Listen, I've truly got to go.'

'Yeah. Guess you have at that. I'll be there, Zimmerman.'

'I'll go, then.'

'Sure. If'n all this turns out well for us, then I'll come and talk to you again.'

'Be careful, Mister Herne. You don't know what it is you're running yourself against.'

'Maybe I do, Mister Zimmerman,' replied Jed, grinning at the little man. 'Maybe I do.'

Herne watched the manager of Mount Morgoth scurry off down the valley through the dawn, the sound of his going quickly muffled by the river. Then he turned back towards the town and began to climb up the hill towards the Sowren mansion, confident that nobody had seen his secret meeting.

He would have been somewhat less confident if he had spotted the gleam of light from one of the upstairs windows of the big house. The sort of flash you get from glass or from polished metal.

From something like, for instance, a powerful telescope.

CHAPTER SEVEN

The day had passed quietly. He had ridden out with the sheriff again, taking in a loop all around the town. Making sure that the trip took in the area eleven miles north and west of the town. Allaying any suspicions that Daley might have had by hurrying through the region, pretending he wanted to get back to the house for the evening meal.

It was a desolate area. Drowned Squaw Canyon was steep-sided, about six hundred paces in length, with half a dozen spur trails coming into it from either side. Most of them clearly blind, but one or two showing signs of having been ridden by men on horseback. One of them in particular looked as though it had been covered very recently. Within the last couple of days.

The weather was cold and both men rode hunched in the saddle, keeping conversation to a minimum. Daley reined in when they were halfway along the canyon and faced Jed.

'Seems to me you aren't exactly burning a hole in your ass trying to track down these sons of bitches, Herne. My opinion, you understand.'

'Guess you're entitled to it, Sheriff. I got a job and I think about it and I do what I think the folks hirin' me want me to do.'

He managed to lay just enough emphasis on the words for the sheriff to catch his drift. The plump lawman laughed heartily.

'Thought you was a clever bastard, Herne. Thought it.'

'I try.'

'Guess you do. Guess you do, Mister Herne. Get to learn the side of your bread carries the butter, don't you? Huh?'

Jed smiled and dug his heels into his stallion's flanks, not replying. Sheriff Daley laughed again and walked his own horse on behind him.

The next day, Herne hung around the house. Cleaning his guns. Stripping and oiling them. Making sure his ammunition was where it should be. Unloading the long fifty calibre Sharps rifle. Wiping it down and pulling through a strip of clean rag. Squinting along the sights to ensure the gun hadn't taken a knock.

The kind of action there was likely to be during the promised silver robbery could lead to the rifle coming in very useful. With its classic rainbow trajectory it wasn't impossible for a good shot to knock a man off his horse at seven or eight hundred paces. And there were cases on record of the Sharps being effective at twice that range.

The Colt was stripped totally down. Like any man out on the frontier who relied for his living and for his life on his gun, Herne carried a complete set of tools with him. A habit he'd learned in the turbulent years after the War from the notorious gunsmith Jack Ryker. A man who turned his skill in helping men by repairing guns into using those guns for killing men for bounties. He always carried a pouch of tools, including some handmade and razor-edged scalpels. Herne had once heard about the time he'd cut off a man's lower lip before he could even draw his pistol. Holding it between finger and thumb of his left hand and making the hissing cut with the right.

Jed relied on the Civil War bayonet in his boot for that kind of action.

After he'd washed and dried the pistol, he carefully polished each component with a soft rag, reassembling the Colt in a little over two minutes. Checking the triple clicking action. Sliding in each round and testing the smoothness of the cylinder.

Out of habit he drew the long, slim-bladed knife from its sheath and ran his thumb along the edge, holding i up to the light from the window to make sure there was no trace of damaging rust. Pressing the tip of a finger against the needle-point.

He was about as ready as he could be.

At the evening meal he pretended that he was suffering from a disposition of the stomach and begged to be excused. Miss Eliza was concerned, her small eyes glinting at him from over the top of the pince-nez that she habitually wore once the light became poor. Her sister was more involved in filling her mouth with a monstrous morsel of roasted turkey, well larded with rich sauce, the plate almost cracking into splinters beneath the weight of a positive mountain of sweet potatoes.

'I trust that this will not prevent your carrying out your duties on our behalf, Mister Herne,' said Eliza, the chill in her voice freezing the air out of the long, gloomy dining-room.

'I trust not, Ma'am,' he replied, bowing his way out into the hall. 'But if I am indisposed then I surely hope you will dock my money on account of it.'

'I will, Mister Herne. I will indeed.' Then, with a rare flash of warmth. 'I do hope that you will be recovered on the morrow.'

'And I, sister,' added Lily, gurgling uncomfortably as she swallowed more in one mouthful than a normal person would eat at an entire sitting.

The next morning Herne rose at his usual time, but again pretended to be ill. Occasionally clutching at his stomach and groaning. Biting his lips as if he were making a considerable effort to fight off the discomfort. It was odd that both the sisters seemed more worried about him that day than they had the previous evening. For some reason they seemed very much to want him better.

It crossed his mind that it might just possibly have something to do with the robbery that Zimmerman had said was coming off that evening. In those situations, it was at least conceivable that someone might want to ensure that they had a careful tab on him so that they knew where he was. A sick man in his room with the door firmly bolted could be anywhere.

Lily persuaded him to come down after lunch to join her again at the piano. Though he had eaten nothing himself, Jed was easily able to deduce what the ladies had lunched on. There were traces of every course splattered across Miss Lily's dress. A vegetable soup. What he suspected must have been buffalo stew from the coarseness of the meat fibres in the folds of the pink satin. And also from the way she kept picking at the rotting remnants of her teeth to dislodge stubborn fragments. The dessert had clearly been some kind of milk pudding.

'Will you join me, Jedediah, in "*I Sowed The Seeds Of Love*"? It is a most beautiful melody.'

They all were before Lily Sowren set her vocal cords to them. She generally used the same book. Published in London, England, by Macmillan, nearly twenty years earlier. Bound in maroon leather and embossed with gold. Herne was coming to hate its glossy appearance. And to hate the compiler of the volume, John Hulla, Professor of Vocal Music in King's College, London, England.

But it was all part of the price that he had to pay.

'You are of course, a Republican, Mister Herne?' asked Eliza, pausing in the doorway. He noticed she was wearing her outdoor clothes. Through the window he could see that it was so overcast that rain could not be far off.

'Of course, Ma'am? And yourself?'

'I would have hardly imagined that a man of your apparent intelligence would have found such a question to be necessary.'

He nodded at the reproof. 'Though I hear that there are some who say that Mister Grover Cleveland for those Democrats has hopes of being elected.'

'Bah! Stuff and nonsense!! If the day ever comes when there is to be another of those fools in the highest office in the land, then I hope that I am not here on this earth to see it.'

With that she swept out, calling back over her shoulder to Lily to make sure that Mister Herne took that sleeping draught. It was the first that Jed had heard of it and he felt his hackles rising.

But the song was coming and it took all of his concentration to avoid Lily Sowren's greasy pawing and her sly, whispered questions about topics that no lady should be concerned with.

'*My garden was planted full*
Of flowers everywhere,
But for myself I could not choose
The flower I held so dear.'

As she warbled on, Jed wondered what the rest of the day

would bring. It was often the case when you were a shootist: that you knew the sunset would mean you had lived through another day of danger. This promised to be another of those days.

Lily Sowren was nearing the end of the maudlin ballad.

'*My garden is now run wild,*
When I shall plant anew,
My bed, that once was filled with thyme
Is over-run with rue,
Yes, 't'is over-run with rue.'

Two hours later, Lily Sowren crept into the room alongside Jed Herne's bedroom and slipped back a small panel behind a picture. Applying her eyes to the hole that was revealed.

As she watched, she began to smile, licking her lips at what she saw. Herne, only half-clothed, was stretched out on his bed, lying there on his back. One boot on, while the other lay on the floor. As though sleep had overtaken him while he was still getting ready for a nap.

'Good,' she whispered. Looking at the helpless man. She knew that Eliza's draughts would keep him unconscious until the next morning and leave him with a foul headache. He would recall very little. Simply that he had been fatigued. That was all.

It was an overwhelming temptation for the fat old woman. Though past forty, Herne's body was in marvellous condition. Well-muscled, the flat stomach and broad shoulders. Lily looked for a long time at the sleeping figure. Trying to pluck up the courage to do something that she knew her dominant and efficient younger sister would take exception to. And when Eliza took exception to something...

'No,' she said, firmly, nearly sliding the peep-panel closed. Then hesitating again, Her right hand falling to her bosom. Then lower.

And lower.

Lower.

Jed kept his eyes closed for another ten minutes, then risking a glance from lowered lids. His position on the bed, seemingly casual and accidental, was the result of a lot of thought. He'd taken the precaution of checking out the room as soon as he had first been left alone in it. Finding the hidden panel behind a picture and another in the corridor wall. From where he had arranged himself on the bed, he could see both while his own eyes remained in shadow. He had seen the movement behind the portrait of a Spanish nobleman, real eyes replacing the canvas ones. Heard the panting, and guessed immediately that it was Lily. Suspecting that she wouldn't dare to spy on him like that for so long if Eliza had been in the house. Taking care to lie very still on the bed. Praying that she wouldn't come in on him, to test by touch if the sleeping-draught had worked. He wasn't sure just how strong his self-control was.

But she went away. Lying still, Herne could hear her heavy lumbering steps as she disappeared into her own room along the corridor. The slam of the door. Even the rattle of the sets of bolts and chains that kept Lily's privacy.

It wasn't the only locked room in the mansion. He'd been exploring all over the rambling house and discovered that some of the cellars were also locked. More heavily locked than he would have thought necessary. The one sure thing in Wild Rose was that nobody would dare to steal from the Misses Sowren.

Finally, when he thought it might be safe, Jed rolled over

and cautiously stood up. He'd only taken a couple of sips from the crystal glass of emerald liquid that Lily had handed him, but it was enough to make his head feel as though he'd been on the liquor for several nights running. What he'd have felt like if he'd drunk the whole glass didn't bear thinking on.

It had been easy to distract the ample Miss Lily while he poured the remainder of the drink into a large potted plant. With olive-green leaves and a rubbery stem. He wondered in passing what the elixir would do to the plant.

Now it was time to be moving.

He blessed the designer of the mansion as he eased his way through his bedroom window, out onto a sturdy trellis that held a rambling tangle of ivy. Sure that it would take his weight as he'd tested it a couple of nights earlier against just such an emergency.

The stable was at the back and he saddled up his stallion, walking it quietly out, straight into a grove of trees that clustered close to the side wall. He thought as he sneaked away that those trees were evidence of how safe most whites now felt against the threat of Indian attack. That grove of leafy trees would have sheltered a hundred Oglala warriors and their ponies.

There was a narrow draw running close beyond the trees and he was soon safely out of sight of the house, swinging himself up into the saddle with an easy grace.

Taking a back trail that would lead him to Drowned Squaw Canyon.

As he heeled the horse onwards, he felt the first pattering spots of rain on the shoulders of his shirt.

By the time he'd covered three miles at an easy canter, the rain had begun to fall in earnest, soaking through the dry ground and converting sand into mud. His slicker was in one of the saddle-bags and he'd pulled it on, though he hated riding in the noisy, constricting, uncomfortable coat.

The sky was dark and he wondered how the time was going. With no sun it was difficult to calculate. He pulled down the brim of his black hat and water tipped from the front, mingling with the rest of the rain on the horse's mane. He was glad that the new guns worked just as well in this kind of weather. He had bitter memories of wet powder and constant misfires during the Civil War.

Zimmerman had said late afternoon. The storm was slowing him down and he knew he was at risk of being too late. But the weather must also be slowing down the wagons with the ore from Old Number One mine. Probably slowing down the robbers as well. It wasn't safe to try and push on faster. There was no knowing where the ambush would be and it would be a dangerous exercise to gallop around a blind corner and find yourself facing armed men.

The rain eased for a few minutes, and then suddenly began to pound down with redoubled power. Lightning came forking across, shattering off the wet rocks around Herne, and it was all that he could do to control his horse, terrified by the new violence of the storm.

Blinking against the flashes of dazzling silver light that spread across the dark sheet of the sky, Herne dismounted and tugged his horse into the cover of a shelf of overhanging rocks. Fighting for breath against the downpour. Patting the terrified animal on the neck to try and calm it. Hanging on the bridle, talking to the stallion all the time. Blowing gently in its nostrils, a trick he'd learned from the Indians.

Winning the battle.

The storm passed as quickly as it had appeared, the black

clouds scudding off towards the south, leaving a land that streamed water from every crevice of stone. The trail had become a ribbon of mud and twice Herne had to urge the horse on through narrow creeks that had instantly become turbulent, bubbling streams in the flash flood. Mud rose as high as the stirrups on one occasion and he wondered what the rain must have done to the Clearwater if it had reached that area. With a localised downpour, it might not even have affected the river.

It took another half hour to reach the end of Drowned Squaw Canyon. During the visit to the area with Sheriff Daley, Jed had seen there was a natural plateau halfway along, up a box canyon, that commanded a view of most of the main trail, and he headed the horse towards it. Hoping he was going to be in time.

He wasn't.

Herne heard the fusillade of shots when he was still a quarter mile short of where he'd wanted to be. And that meant a change of plan. By the time he reached the vantage point, the robbers could be well hidden from him. Maybe driving off the wagons to a chosen spot before they transferred the ore to mules.

'Come on you bastard,' he hissed at his mount, giving it a punch between the ears that made it stagger, kicking in the spurs at the same time. Hanging on the reins with one hand while he drew the heavy Sharps with the other.

When he heard more shots he pulled in on the reins, bringing the horse rearing on its hind legs in protest at the treatment. This time the shooting was different. Several spaced shots. Six, he counted. At regular intervals.

Jed slipped from the stallion's back and tethered it quickly to a spur of wet rock, just out of sight of the main trail through the canyon. Peeling off the slicker he walked quickly, splashing through puddles, pausing at the next corner of the canyon and peering around it, the cocked rifle in his hands.

It was the sort of scene that he'd feared. A scene that he'd seen many times in different places with only minor changes to it. Sometimes it had been a civilian wagon filled with women and children. And the attackers had been red. Apache or Sioux, most times. Sometimes the wagon had been a military one, with supplies or ammunition. Once or twice a stage with masked killers around it. Once it had even been a wagon train attacked by other whites, with scenes of the most appalling butchery. That had been at the time of the worst of the Mormon troubles.

This time, it was three wagons. With what looked like had once been two men guarding each one. They weren't doing any guarding now.

They were all dead, and Jed recognised the meaning of those half dozen, spaced, careful shots. The bright blood showed up in the dim light, and he could see that each man had been shot several times. Mostly in the body, the close grouping of the wounds showing that their slayers hadn't been far away. But each corpse also had another wound. A dark-rimmed hole in the middle of the forehead, directly between the eyes. Powder burns showing the shots had been fired with the muzzle of the guns touching the skin. The silver robbers were very careful and professional men. They knew that the price of silence was high, but cheaply bought with a bullet through the brain. The best witness was a dead witness.

And the best robber was a dead one, thought Jed, checking their numbers.

Four. Again, that meant his original thoughts about the hi-jacking were right. To get that close to a half dozen edgy guards, meant that they had found some way of taking the men by surprise. That meant a trick, or maybe that they knew them. A man you know can kill you a whole lot easier than a stranger. Just depends on what you're expecting.

Four robbers.

One already hefting the bodies from the seats of the canvas-topped wagons. One more holding the horses. On foot. A third was at the back of the furthest rig, starting to unlace the cover. The fourth man looked like the leader. He was a big man, sitting his bay mare a little apart from the others. Directing the operation. There was something familiar about the man's shape.

That could come later. Right now Herne's only worry was the simplest way of shooting down four men and killing them without risking his own life.

There was the question of which one to take first.

Not the leader. A man in the saddle when shooting began was at a disadvantage, with his mount bucking under him.

Same applied to the robber holding the horses. Who also seemed a touch familiar, Herne thought. Though the light was so poor in the deeps of the canyon that it was hard to make anything out. That man would also find himself busy when the other three horses all began to kick as the shooting began.

That left two.

One behind the wagon. The other on the seat, tipping off corpses as calmly as if he was shifting sacks of flour in a main street store.

'One behind the rig,' breathed Jed, cocking the long rifle, putting a dab of spit on the foresight to help show up his target in the gloom. Cuddling the gun against himself, finger on the trigger, stock rammed hard into his shoulder.

One of the men . . . the burly figure on horseback, shouted something to the man behind the wagon who called back, his head appearing round the corner.

It couldn't have been better.

At such comparatively short range, Herne could have taken the pips off a playing card. Striking a man through the middle of the skull was like shooting fish in a barrel.

The boom of the gun echoed around the rocks, and for a moment the target was obscured by the cloud of black powder smoke that billowed out of the muzzle. During the next six seconds, several things happened at once.

The horses all reared up at once at the unexpected noise. The heavily-built man coming close to being unseated as he fought for control, drawing his pistol and dropping it again as he clung to the reins. The man with the horses was also having problems. All three of them were bucking and rearing and he dived out of the way, letting go of the bridles, rolling in the clinging mud, screaming to the others for help.

The man on the seat was unlucky.

He was just standing up, balancing against the movement of the rig, a corpse draped in his arms like a dance-hall whore. The noise of the Sharps and the screaming of the man in the dirt all combined to spook the horses drawing the wagons. They started forwards, sending him toppling sideways off the seat, the weight of the body making it impossible for him to save himself.

He landed awkwardly and Herne clearly heard the brittle snap of a bone breaking, above the bedlam of other noises, as the leg folded under the killer, leaving him helpless.

That was three of them.

And the fourth?

He was dead.

Extremely dead.

A heavy bullet, like a fifty calibre, hitting a man in the head is likely to kill him. And this particular murderer was no exception. It hit him a finger's width above his left eye as he looked out at his leader. Making a neat hole through the frontal bone of the temples, carrying on into the soft puddle of brains. Its pointed shape was a little battered from the impact, and its clean trajectory was distorted so that it had begun to tip end over end. Tearing out an enormous chunk of the pink-grey tissue. Finally exiting like a mighty metal fist through the back of the head. Punching a hole four inches in diameter through which the dying man's brains and blood poured out in a red flood.

The impact was enough to kick him staggering backwards, nerveless fingers letting the wet canvas of the wagon slip from his grip as he fell.

There was little pain. The sensation of the enormous blow on the front of the head, then a white light that blazed ferociously for a fraction of infinity, before the flame burned out into limitless blackness. He didn't feel that he had fallen. Nor the wetness of the mud on his face, soaking up the crimson.

Dying is very easy. The only basic qualification is being alive in the first place.

Herne reloaded the Sharps and selected the next target.

The one on the floor had barely realised what was happening, the first spasms of agony from his smashed leg making him start to scream. A noise that set off the horses into a frenzy of kicking and whinnying. The robber who had been supposed to be holding them had given up on that task, trying to draw his pistol where he knelt in the dirt, spray from the trampling horses blinding him as he peered around for the invisible assassin.

And the leader on the horse hadn't even come close to regaining control of his animal.

Jed shot the kneeling man first, the Sharps being a fine gun on a more or less stationary target, but not so useful as a Winchester on someone in the saddle of a prancing mare.

The bullet hit the man through the top of his head, where he was bowed over trying to wipe his eyes clean. The impact shattered a huge chunk of skull, lifting it clean away in whirling fragments of white bone. Killing him instantly.

This time the reloading took a little longer, his fingers slipping on the wet cartridge. Fumbling it and nearly dropping the gun. Glancing up to see that the leader of the robbers nearly had his bay under control. Yelping something at his crippled colleague, having successfully drawn his other pistol from his belt.

Rather than waste the cocked Sharps, Herne took quick aim and shot the man with the broken leg, the bullet opening up his throat in a welter of choking bubbling scarlet. It was a mercy. Like the mercy you might show a horse with a similar injury. But Jed didn't think of it that way.

He just thought of it as one less bastard for him to worry about.

'Herne!!!' roared the man on horseback, finally managing to get his animal moving in the right direction, snapping off a couple of shots from his hand-gun. Heading in like an avenging angel of death, homing on the cloud of powder smoke that still hung in the damp evening air.

The mark of the great killer is that he rarely has to hurry. And when he does it's with a precise haste, without fumbling or panic. Jed laid the smoking rifle down against the wall of rock at the side of the canyon, and drew the Peacemaker from its holster. Thumbing back on the hammer, aiming up at the man galloping in towards him.

There was a great veil of mud and spray being kicked up by the horse's hooves, mingling with the rain that had again begun to fall with a frightening force, pounding off the rocks and splattering all around Jed's boots.

'Bastard!!' screamed the rider, firing off a cascade of lead in Herne's direction, emptying his pistol before he was within forty paces.

Jed stood very still, hearing the bullets splintering off the boulders, none of them coming within ten feet of him, holding his own gun in his right hand, steadying it as if he was on a target range with his left hand.

Waiting.

His attacker saw his death coming, unable to restrain his mare from bearing him fast towards it. His mouth falling open ready to yell for mercy.

The first bullet hit his horse in the middle of the nose, close up towards its eyes; the second, fired a fraction of a second later, hit the wretched creature in the chest, knocking it off its feet, to topple sideways in a screaming tangle, its fall obscured by the water and slime on the canyon floor.

Jed knew that the horse was dying and paid it no further attention, moving a few steps sideways so that he could get in a straight shot at the rider.

The big man had been thrown clear, lying half on his side a few paces away, struggling to get to his feet, face a mask of dirt-caked horror. Hands reaching out towards the gunman.

As he knelt there, the rain that teemed from the darkening sky washed away the mud and Herne recognised him. Despite the terror, he recognised him. Up to that moment Jed had been about to take him prisoner, to find out the story behind the killings and the thefts.

Now there didn't seem much point.

So he shot Mayor Julius Daley twice through the chest, watching as he rolled over, kicking and coughing, the bright coloured blood diffused to pink by the rain, mingling with the mud and dirt.

When it was done he walked across, reloading as he did so,

kicking the other bodies over to see the faces. Two he vaguely recognised from the town. The third was Hempstead, the clerk, his brains all leaked away in Drowned Squaw Canyon alongside the mayor.

Jed stood in the downpour for some time, wondering about the way the robbery had ended.

'Ended,' he said to nobody in particular. 'Hell, I figure it's not even started.'

CHAPTER EIGHT

It hadn't been how he'd expected it.

'*Shall we gather at the river?*'

Not at all like Herne had thought it might be.

'*The beautiful, the beautiful river?*'

It hadn't been possible to harness up all the teams, so he'd heaved every single one of the bodies in the back of the leading rig, and tied his stallion on behind. Riding it on to Wild Rose City, arriving well after dark.

'*Shall we gather at the river?*'

There had been an incredible commotion and he'd had to fire a couple of shots in the air to hush the crowd that had gathered around the wagon, staring in unbelieving horror at the tangled, mud-sodden bodies. Four of them respected members of the community. Herne hadn't even been sure whether they'd believe him, but there was enough evidence, once he got them to listen to him. The pistols with empty chambers, the bullets matching up with the number of wounds to the guards from the Old Number One ore train.

'*That flows by the throne of God?*'

Only a day later the funerals were taking place in the cemetery behind the Sowren mansion. Fairly quiet occasions for the three commoners and something more grandiose for Julius Daley, mayor and brothel-keeper of Wild Rose City. The entire family were there, as was what seemed like the whole population of the Dakota township.

The rain had come and gone intermittently, turning Main

Street into a slippery trail of grey-orange mud, where the horses fought for a footing as they hauled up the coffins to their last resting place. Many of the mourners also showed streaks of dirt on their best clothes where they'd fallen on their way up.

'Yes, we'll gather at the river,

That flows by the throne of God.'

Even high up above the town, Herne could clearly hear the rumbling of the Clearwater as it surged angrily through its bed. The rains had swollen it to unrecognisable proportions in the last three days, and it now threatened the entire lower part of the town.

At an ordinary time that state of the flooding river would have kept everyone's mind full. But now Wild Rose City had other matters to keep it talking.

Or, perhaps, to keep it silent.

The priest had at last finished, and the burials were over. Jed turned on his heel and began to walk away from the gravesides, when he felt a hand on his arm.

'Mister Herne.'

'Yes?'

The sisters stood close together, side by side. Eliza towering over Lily, both dressed in long trailing dresses, with black bonnets and veils that covered their faces, so he couldn't see more of them than the glittering of their eyes.

'We wish to talk to you again, Mister Herne. When we first heard the tidings of the men you had slain, I confess that we were . . . How shall I put it?'

Lily interrupted her. 'I think we were shocked by it, sister.'

'Yes, shocked.'

'And stunned,' added Lily.

Eliza nodded. 'And stunned.'

In case Herne had missed the point of how they had felt, Lily muttered: 'Yes. Shocked and stunned.'

They had fallen into step with him as they walked towards the house through the rows of grave markers. Herne was uncomfortably aware that the two brothers of Julius Daley were walking behind him. And the Sowren boys behind them. The rest of the congregation seemed to have melted away into the misty air.

'He was a good boy, Julius,' said Eliza. 'Real kind to animals.'

Herne thought of the six dead men with bullet holes leaking their lives away in Drowned Squaw Canyon, and he kept quiet.

'You must have thought we didn't believe you, Mister Herne?' said Lily, her fat hands stuffed into black cotton gloves that gripped at his arm.

'No, Ma'am,' he replied.

That wasn't what he'd thought. They'd appeared on their porch, like strangely distorted images of each other, facing him as he'd walked up the hill with Sheriff Daley. The fat lawman had been silent. Clearly fighting a desire to wipe Jed off the earth with a hail of bullets, but fearing his aunts too much.

They'd listened to him, both watching him, ignoring the small crowd that had clustered around them. Taking no notice at all of the wailing that was coming up as three women in Wild Rose discovered that they were widows and eleven children began to understand about losing fathers.

Neither Eliza nor Lily had said a word to him from that moment on until they followed him from the graves, one each side, like uneven brackets. They had gone into the house and closed the door after he had finished his account of the bloody massacre, leaving him with Sheriff Daley. After three or four minutes a servant had come out with a sealed envelope that he had handed to Jedediah on a silver salver. Inside was a short note.

'Mister Herne. We are distressed by what you have done but we must have time to think about the repercussions that will follow. We wish you to remain in our employ for the present until after the interments then we will discuss the matter further.'

It wasn't signed. It didn't need to be.

Until the burials they had both remained in their rooms and Herne had eaten alone in the dining-room. Seeing and hearing nothing of either of them, though he several times caught raised voices from their rooms. The remaining Daleys and Gawain and Joab Sowren also visited the mansion several times for long discussions with their elderly relations. Once it was Zimmerman who came up, with the lawman to keep him company. Staying so close to the nervous little manager that Herne wondered whether he was actually guarding him.

And now they seemed friends again with him. As near to being friendly as they ever got.

Instead of going into the house, they had walked with him around the garden, pausing by a hand-carved bench that overlooked the town, the valley and the far-off mine.

He noticed that the relations had disappeared into the lowering house, and he was alone with the ladies.

'There,' said Eliza Sowren, sweeping out her arms in an untypically grandiose gesture, embracing the whole horizon, the Black Hills, topped with low cloud, stretching out into the far distance.

'Mighty pretty, Ma'am.'

'It is. I recall when Papa was becoming ill; do you not remember, Lily, how . . .?'

'I do, sister, dear. Indeed I do.'

Again Jed noticed their strange ability to speak to each other without words, as though they knew just what the other was thinking.

'Beg pardon, Miss Sowren,' said Herne. 'But I don't know what you're talking about.'

'Of course,' said Eliza, skittishly, tapping him on the arm with her gloves. 'He brought us both up here and showed us this most wonderful vista and he said to us that one day all of this would belong to us and that we were to cherish it and let nobody ever take it away from us. It is quite beautiful, is it not?'

'It is,' he replied, with absolute honesty, wondering what else they were going to say. Whether they were going to mention his amazing recovery from the illness. Or his disappearance from the room. Or maybe just how he happened to be out there in Drowned Squaw Canyon at the very moment their nephew Julius and three members of the honest citizenry of Wild Rose City were carrying out a heinous robbery and multiple murder.

There were a lot of questions and he didn't have an awful lot of answers.

Still, time was passing and nothing too ghastly had happened. He stood there with the two old ladies, viewing one of the finest horizons it was possible to imagine.

The sun was breaking through the clouds and here and there he could see the shafts of light, like golden spears, cutting down from heaven to earth, reflecting back off the wet rocks of the hills all around.

He could see the white lace of several waterfalls plunging down sheer faces of stone, and make out the misty pounding of the Clearwater far below them. It looked as though the spell of bad weather might be finally coming to its end and spring was going to set her green teeth to the land once more.

'Why?'

He found himself taken aback by the snapped question, coming to his surprise from Lily.

Much of the shock stemming from the fact that 'Why?' wasn't one of the questions that he'd been waiting for from them.

He'd been looking to hear 'Who told you?' or 'How did you know?' But not that flat 'Why?'

'I'm sorry, Miss Lily,' he said, stalling to buy himself time.

'I'm sure you are, Mister Herne, yet strangely my sister and I are not at all sorry.'

'That is correct, Lily,' continued Eliza. 'We are not sorry at all about dear Julius and Mister Hempstead and the other two. Not at all.'

'No?'

'No.'

'Absolutely not sorry. Indeed, Mister Herne, I should go so far as to say that we are pleased that you have so skilfully removed the canker from our midst.'

'Your nephew is dead, Miss Sowren.'

'Yes. And I am pleased ...' she paused and corrected herself. '*We* are pleased, that poor Julius has been checked in his career of evil, and that he will no longer be able to contaminate the good people of our town. It is a blessing that you have so skilfully wielded the surgeon's blade against him.'

Lily nodded to her sister, who continued the same thread of conversation.

'We are delighted. For Julius and the others now sleep in the arms of Almighty God, where there is neither pain nor wickedness. Nor want nor corruption. We are gentle people, my sister and myself, Mister Herne, and we are sorrowful that the evil thing came from a member of our family. But he erred from the straight and narrow path of virtue and you were there as the angel with the blazing sword to steer him back into the fold of sweet Jesus Christ, our Lord.'

'Amen,' said Eliza.

'Amen,' added Jedediah, feeling that it was called for.

'So you can leave tomorrow.'

'What?'

It was as calm and flat a rejection of his services as Jed had ever encountered. Eliza smiled at him icily.

'Yes. You've done what we asked you to do, Mister Herne. Admirably. You have stopped the robberies of silver ore from this part of the Dakota Territory and you have not only tracked down the villains responsible for these outrages . . .'

'You have succeeded in single-handedly slaying them all,' concluded Lily.

'Every one,' added Eliza.

'And so we feel it would be better for you if you were now to leave.'

'And for the town.'

'Pick up the pieces.'

'Heal the scars.'

'Balm upon the suffering.'

'Pay you off.'

'With bonus.'

'Excellent job.'

'Give you references.'

'Of course.'

'Of course,' echoed Lily.

'You are everything that we learned you were, Mister Herne,' smiled Eliza, chilling him with her approbation.

'Everything.'

'And more.'

'Indeed, sister. Everything, and so very much more.'

It was unnerving. Like watching a ball being bounced very fast between two children, and Herne felt his head spinning.

'So you want me out?'

It wasn't quite the phrase that he'd intended to use, but it conveyed the flavour of what he meant even better. Jed could see that by the look that flashed between the sisters.

'We don't understand what you mean, Mister Herne,' said Lily Sowren.

'Are you implying that we have . . . ?'

'I'm not sayin' nothing, Ma'am. Just that I see you want me out of the way.'

'What?'

'So's you can get on with bringin' this pretty little town back to something like it was. That's all I mean to say.'

The temperature between them rose by twenty degrees. They both looked in at him and favoured him with a smile. Though he felt that there was something going on between them. That they were speaking to each other and that they were both pleased with what he'd said.

'Of course. Will you be able to leave today?'

'I guess I'd like to stay one more night with you, if that's not too tough. And make a fresh, bright start first thing at dawn.'

'Excellent. We will dine together and then you can retire early. I'm sure you don't want to go running about on your last night with us.'

Herne wasn't sure whether that was a simple statement or whether there was the shadow of a threat lurking somewhere behind it.

Either way, it didn't matter much. He was going to do what he wanted to do, anyway.

He found the note when he returned to his room. In the rush and bustle around the graves, someone had managed to get close enough to him to push it into a jacket pocket. It was obvious who it was.

'*It's not over and you've touched the top that's all and it's got to be stop or it's for nothing and I will tell you tonight.*'

There wasn't a signature.

Didn't need to be. Jed recognised the frightened scribble of Robert Zimmerman, mine manager. He was careful to take the note and slip it beneath the flower-decorated chamber-pot under the bed, knowing it would be safe there until the next morning.

He was so careful that he was inexcusably careless.

So involved in the hiding-place that he never noticed the eyes of the painting on the wall. Not canvas eyes.

Flickering human eyes!

CHAPTER NINE

The food was excellent.

The Sowrens and the Daleys managed to put on a good show of hospitality towards the man who had killed Julius. Keeping up with the idea that they were relieved that Herne had come along to Wild Rose City and lanced the swelling of evil and corruption that had festered for so long, invisible and unsuspected in their midst.

The ladies were better at it than the men, who found it harder to veil their hostility. Jed could see anger lurking in their eyes, beneath the mask of light conversation.

But the jarring note was struck by Zimmerman.

Herne could hardly believe that the little man was going to survive the evening. There were great grey bags under his eyes, and he coughed constantly. Blinking so fast that it was obviously a nervous tic, and he hardly said a word all during the meal, unless he was directly addressed by either of the old ladies. His suit was crumpled and stained and his hair matted and greasy. He looked as if he hadn't slept for a week. He carefully avoided even looking at Herne, toying with the food on his plate and sipping at the red wine in the crystal goblet at his elbow.

Jed realised that it would be difficult for them to snatch a few moments of private conversation. He was sensitive to atmosphere – it went with the job – and he was conscious that they were both being watched. He guessed that the Misses Sowren must have realised that someone had tipped him off about their nephew and his gang of desperadoes, and that someone just might have been Zimmerman. But they could only be suspicions. They couldn't have any proof.

By now his own thoughts, ridiculous as they had at first appeared, were hardening to an amazing near certainty.

The whole family must be involved. It was obvious that the two old ladies took no active part, but they must have had their own ideas about what their nephew had been doing. Herne guessed that the ladies simply closed their eyes to it and pretended it would go away. Doubtless they had been genuinely shocked when he had presented them with such irrefutable proof of Julius's wickedness.

His personal feeling was that Sheriff Daley was probably the prime mover in a conspiracy, and he also suspected that his brother and both the Sowren boys were in on it. If they'd shut their eyes to their nephews, it followed that Eliza and Lily would not want to know about Gawain and Joab.

All he could do was sit tight and watch. The whole atmosphere of Wild Rose was getting to him. Its prim and clean exterior, hiding the Lord only knew what secret sins and black cruelty. The first impression had been washed away by his time there and he felt a great temptation to do what he'd said. He'd been paid. They were happy. All he had to do was pack his saddle-bags and ride out on his stallion at dawn.

And never look back.

The evening finished early. After they had listened to Miss Lily punishing popular songs for an hour, both ladies stood, one resplendent in pink, the other in purple, and announced that they were retiring.

Zimmerman stood with the rest of them, looking wildly round the room as if he was hoping for an avenue of escape. Eliza caught the glance and smiled at him.

'You will stay here for the night, Robert.'

'Oh, but . . .'

'I shall hear no "buts" from you. I insist. You can have the east room, beyond mine. I will instruct the servants to air the bed for you.' Seeing his mouth gaping open. 'No protests, now. You know that we have always been a big happy family, Robert. You will stay.'

The smile stayed there, glued in place. But the golden glow of the polished oil lamps was not enough to illuminate the deeps of her eyes, perched uneasily astride the top of her bony nose.

Herne watched Zimmerman, trembling like a rabbit before a rattler, swaying on his feet as if he was about to faint.

After the sisters had withdrawn, Sheriff Daley turned to the manager and patted him on the back. 'You and me got the room with a connectin' door, Bob. Now ain't that real cosy. Why don't you an' me go up now and we can jaw some about life before sleepin'? If you others'll excuse us . . .'

'I wanted to go for a walk, Sheriff,' stammered Zimmerman. 'I always like the view from the cemetery wall across the valley at midnight. Really like that . . . like it a whole lot. Midnight, by that wall. Real pretty . . .'

He finally looked at Herne, making the assignation even more clear. If he'd written it large upon a sheet of card and walked around the room with it, the meeting-place and time couldn't have been more obvious. Jed guessed that it was born from fear and desperation, seeing that the family was going to keep him from seeing the shootist, cribbing him up until after he'd ridden away.

But none of the men seemed to notice, simply bidding each other their goodnights. Joab and Gawain offering Herne a last cigar from a silver humidor on the sideboard. Which he refused, retiring to his own room and bolting the door. Checking that the note was undisturbed. It was still there.

Getting on the bed, fully clothed, and lying back in the darkness, waiting for midnight.

From his room he could see the garden. See the rough stone of the graveyard wall. Staring at it in the white light of the moon, he recalled a song he'd once heard a whore sing in a bar in Memphis. Pretty girl with a knife-scar around her mouth. '*Why build a wall round a graveyard, when nobody wants to get in? Why build a wall round a graveyard, when nobody wants to get out?*'

Funny how that had come back to him at such a moment.

He'd heard the noise of movement along the corridors, better than an hour after he'd gone to his own room. Men talking in low voices. A scuffling sound, that stopped very quickly.

At that point Jed had climbed into the bed, simply pulling the blankets over him, keeping on all his clothes, the Colt ready drawn and cocked in his right hand. It seemed like a time for being careful.

There was the faintest scraping of noise, somewhere behind the wall. Like a mouse lurking at the back of a curtain. Half on his side Jed tried to see into the darkness. He had excellent night vision and he had learned from the Chiricahua Apache the trick of looking slightly to one side of something in poor light to get a better sight of it.

But the room was fully dark.

Or was there the hint of something halfway along ...? Behind the picture? A trace of a glow where the eyes of the picture should be?

A glow that vanished as soon as he thought he'd seen it.

Remembering that hidden spy-hole made him suddenly concerned about hiding the message from Zimmerman. Maybe they'd seen him and found it. Replaced it. Maybe.

If they had, then the manager was a dead man, and so was he.

'If you got a choice of standing and being killed and moving and being killed, then get moving.' He couldn't remember who'd said that to him. It was probably Whitey Coburn, the lean albino who'd shared so many of his adventures. Sounded like Whitey.

It was good advice and Herne followed it. Slipping from the bed and out down the trellis, into the moon-bathed garden.

It was empty, the town beneath silent and black. Used to frontier settlements where the drinking and womanising went from dawn to dusk and round again to dawn, Herne found this orderliness eerie and unnatural. He strode through the damp grass to the wall near the cemetery, in case Zimmerman had somehow managed to elude his guards. For that was what the Sowrens and Daleys were. Jed no longer had much doubt about that. Even though he excluded the two old ladies from that judgement.

There was nobody there. The garden was still and deserted, just a light wind blowing through the topmost branches of the trees. He looked back at the house, wondering if he was being observed, but not a light shone anywhere.

'Hey,' he breathed to himself, seeing a dim strip of gold against the midnight mansion. A vertical line of light that seemed to be coming from somewhere near the level of the grass. That meant it must be in one of the cellars. Maybe in one of those heavily-bolted underground chambers.

Herne stepped like a great panther, the long wet grass of the lawn muffling every sound of his boots. The pistol again drawn and cocked in his right hand. Probing at the darkness before him like a lethal antenna.

As he came nearer he could see that one of the massive wooden shutters across the window had warped a little in the recent rain, leaving a gap no more than a half inch wide.

Finally, he was against it, pressed close to the wall of the house. In a pool of deep shadow. Finger on the trigger, Herne edged in, closing one eye so that he could see through the gap, into the brightly-lit cellar beyond.

In his life Jed Herne had seen more dreadful things than most men could ever even imagine. Seen death and injury in a hundred places. Inflicted more than his share of it. And in the end it ceased to mean as much. You became less sensitive to it. You grew an extra skin so that you didn't go mad when you saw what was left of a close friend after Arapaho squaws had been sporting with him for three long, long days. It was the only way to be.

He thought he'd seen about everything there was for a man to see.

But he'd never imagined anything like he saw in the cellar of the house of Miss Eliza and Miss Lily Sowren in the town of Wild Rose in Dakota Territory in that mild spring night of eighteen hundred and eighty-five.

It was like something from a vision of Hell, painted by a madman. And from outside the mansion, there wasn't a lot he could do. Just watch.

And listen. The window had been opened to let in a breath of air and he could hear snatches of the conversation through the gap in the shutters.

Above the noise of the fire and the muffled groans and screams of Robert Zimmerman.

What was left of him.

*

From where he was Herne could see most of the small cellar. See the great oak door with its studded metal bolts. An iron grille in it, making it like a prison. The walls were of rough stone, with various rings set fast in them at differing heights. At the centre of the one wall was a fire-basket, filled with glowing coals. So hot they gave out a shimmering white light. In the brazier Jed could see several rods of odd lengths and shapes. Like branding irons.

In the middle of the room, more or less beneath the window where he watched, Herne could see an oak table. About six feet in length, with its sturdy legs bolted to the floor. There were odd stains along its length. Dark brown, almost black, that he would have wagered his life were dried blood. Old dried blood.

And on it were sets of tools. Whips of varying lengths. Some with braided leather thongs. Some with cruel metal tips vicious enough to tear the skin from a man's back in a dozen lashes. And there were knives. Long, broad-bladed cleavers like a butcher's, and narrow daggers with points like needles. There were hooked implements and devices for probing and rending and stretching. A handful of silver pins and lengths of new hemp rope, some thick and some thin.

At each corner of the table he noticed a set of iron manacles, with heavy locks on them.

But what caught the eye more were the three people in the room.

One man and two women.

Eliza Sowren. Lily Sowren.

And their manager, Robert Zimmerman.

Herne blinked twice to make sure that he wasn't locked in some appalling nightmare. But he wasn't. What was going on in that sweltering cellar was hideously real.

*

Zimmerman was naked.

His body was stretched out against the stone wall in a cross shape. Wrists chained to rings high up, near the ceiling, drawing him up so that his feet hardly touched the floor. His ankles were also spread as wide as possible, secured with more chains. The flickering light of the fire cast shimmering shadows across his skin. throwing parts of his body momentarily into darkness.

There was a collar of metal around the small man's neck, secured to a great bolt above his head, holding him quite still and helpless.

Herne stood motionless in the dark pool of shadow by the house wall and watched. The only movement the heaving of his chest and the tightening of his hand around the butt of the Colt, the knuckles bone-white in the night.

Miss Eliza and Miss Lily moved around the cellar as calmly as if they were holding an afternoon tea for a few of their respectable friends. Eliza wore a silk dress in her favourite purple, and Lily was predictably in pink. The macabre touch was that both of them were wearing gloves to above the elbows. Both in colours that matched their dresses.

Lily was sweating furiously in the heat, pausing to wipe her forehead. Herne noticed then that both the women were dappled with spots of blood. And that Lily's pink gloves were sodden with crimson around both hands, clear up to the wrists.

It didn't take a lot of imagination to see what was going on. To know the reason for the hideous torture of the wretched Zimmerman.

Faintly through the shutters, Jed heard the muttered conversation.

'You'd do well to tell us the whole truth, Robert, my dear young boy.'

That was Eliza.

'All of this will stop as soon as we believe what you are telling us. The pain will go away and you can go and sleep and get better.'

That was Lily, smiling across at her younger sister.

'Told you. Said where robbery was. When. Nothing else. Swear I didn't. Not you. He doesn't know 'bout you. I swear it.' Herne was puzzled by the garbled tone to the manager's voice, as if he was having difficulty speaking. He pressed his eye closer to the gap and was able to make out the details of what the two respectable ladies had done to their helpless victim.

They must have been working on him for more than an hour to have achieved so much.

There were burn marks around his face, threads of blood worming from his eyes, his nose and his ears. There was more congealing blood around the mouth. By straining, Herne could see Zimmerman's feet, and understood why he was finding talking so difficult. One or both of the Misses Sowren had carefully knocked out every tooth from his mouth, leaving them on the floor in front of him.

There were more burns across his hairless chest, patches of bright crimson around each nipple showing where the sharp knives had been employed. There were no nails left on either fingers or toes.

Weals across his chest and the lower part of his stomach showed clearly where he had been savagely whipped, some of the bloody marks extending to his genitals. His body was splattered with vomit and from the bitter stench, Jed could tell that the wretched manager had fouled himself, either from shock or from pain.

'Better tell us, you naughty boy,' giggled Lily, stepping in closer, seizing him by the genitals. Twisting and clutching them with agonising force, making his mouth sag open in a silent scream. Lily was panting with enjoyment of what she was doing, wrenching at his body harder, using her great weight, face close to Zimmerman's, savouring every exquisite second of his suffering.

'He'll have another fit of the vapours if you do that for too long, sister,' called Eliza. 'Then we won't find out what the stinking little whoreson told that shootist, Herne.'

Lily reluctantly relinquished her prize, slapping him hard across the face to restore him to consciousness. She was as strong as any man, and the blows from her gloved fist rocked the little man's head from side to side, the crack of the blows clearly audible to Herne outside the house.

Eliza had picked up a metal spike from the fire. It was about fourteen inches long, and she held it with a thick cloth to protect her fingers from the obvious heat. The tip was about an inch wide, but it quickly widened to the breadth of a man's forearm. She held it up so that Zimmerman could see it, laughing as he whimpered. Guessing through the red mist of pain what she intended to do with it. What part of his body was going to be ravaged and abused by the hot iron.

'Please, don't ... Please!! I can't tell you any more!!!'

'Yes you can, my sweet boy,' said Lily, so quietly that Jed could hardly hear her. 'You can tell us so much more. But not too quickly.'

She was flushed with the exertions, swaying on her feet, eyes shutting in a kind of grotesque rapture, while Eliza closed in with the metal spike, ready to impale their victim.

'Tell us, Bobby,' said Eliza. 'Just tell us what that murdering son of a bitch upstairs knows. Then it'll stop for you.'

'I've told ... told you what I know.'

She drew nearer to him and Herne began to level the pistol, intending to shoot both women down in cold blood.

Not that his blood was cold. It boiled with a relentless anger at the evil women, seeing now that he had been wrong all along. It wasn't the sons or the nephews that were behind the robberies and the killings. It was simply these two respectable silver-haired old ladies.

'After that I'll get the hot spoon and take out his eyes, sister, dear,' said Lily.

'Perhaps we can cook them up for him. I fear he's going to be with us for some time before he comes to his senses and he will become hungry.'

'Only one eye, sister,' smiled Lily. 'We would not want him to avoid seeing what is happening to him. That would be a great cruelty, surely?'

Eliza moved in closer with the long metal bar in her hand, approaching Zimmerman, who was writhing in his chains.

'Can you open his legs a little wider for me, sister?' she asked.

'Perhaps if I can reach high enough to kick him. Or if we slice off this pathetic little pizzle of his,' Lily said, grabbing at him again, making his head roll from side to side in pain.

'Slice that off and feed it to him a piece at a time. Like cutting gristle off a fine steak.'

Lily reached for one of the gleaming blades from the blood-stained table, laughing with delight at the prospect of what they were going to do.

Herne's blazing anger had gone. Replaced by an icy bitterness. Tainted with a sickness to the pit of his stomach at what was happening.

It was time to end it.

He brought the Peacemaker up in his right hand, levelling it at Eliza Sowren through the bright segment of light. Ready to kill her.

When there was a flash of pain across the back of his own skull. The dark pool of shadow where he'd been hiding seemed to rise up his body and swallow him in its black depths.

CHAPTER TEN

Recovering consciousness was generally more painful than being knocked out. The pain was what brought you round. Grinding, tearing pain. Feeling as though the back of the head had been torn apart.

When Jed came to he was facing a pair of bright oil lamps, both turned up so high that the glass chimneys were becoming fast blackened with soot. The flames flickered and danced, throwing strange shadows across the walls and ceiling.

It is impossible to disguise the fact that you are coming round. At that time there is no way at all that you can control your body. The eyes flicker and there are involuntary movements that you can do nothing about.

'He's back!' called a voice that sounded as though it came from the further end of a railroad tunnel. Sounded like Marcus Daley, the saloon-keeper, but with his eyes still squeezed shut against that light, Jed didn't bother to look round to see.

It didn't make a whole lot of difference. It didn't matter either who had slugged him, creeping silently up through the muffling long grass as he prepared to gun down Eliza and Lily.

None of that mattered.

He heard the sound of feet moving in towards him. One man. A light woman, tapping along on elevated heels. And the ponderous tread that must be Lily Sowren. Despite his great reserves of courage, Herne felt a pang of what must have been fear at the thought that he was helpless in the power of those two unspeakably wicked old women.

There was the crack of a boot in the ribs and he rolled over on his side. Testing the rawhide thongs that bound him. They'd done a good job. His wrists were forced tightly together behind his back, the cords cutting into his skin. He couldn't feel his fingers, and guessed that the nails would be swollen and black from the pressure of the bindings. His ankles were also tied, though not so efficiently. Moving his leg he could feel that they hadn't found the razored bayonet in its sheath in his right boot. It seemed to be the only card he held against the royal flush of the Misses Sowren.

Outside he could hear the sound of the wind, beginning to rise suddenly as if a storm threatened. Herne doubted whether he'd live to see it.

Rolling over also brought home to him the fact that there was a narrow cord linking his wrists to his throat. If he attempted any sudden movement then he was likely to strangle himself.

'Do take care with yourself, Mister Herne,' said Eliza Sowren.

Jed squinted up at her, seeing her elongated form stretching out far above him, the angle making her look more than ten feet tall.

'Yes, Mister Herne. We have no wish to harm you any further,' added Lily, standing at the side of her sister.

Herne kept his mouth shut. There didn't seem a lot he could say.

'Conversation will, regrettably, have to be brief. You have stumbled upon our secret, and the price for that comes very high.'

'Extremely high,' added Lily.

'What have you done with Zimmerman?' asked Jed, feeling at the thongs holding him, deciding that they had been tied too tightly for him to hope to shift them.

'My sons have taken him back to the mine,' replied Eliza. 'He was very foolish, was he not? Now we shall see him no more.'

'What about the body?' Surely the whole damned town and the workers at the mine couldn't all be involved in the murders and thefts.

'Smelting furnace gets mighty hot, Mister Herne,' laughed Marcus Daley, with a fat man's throaty chuckle.

That was it. Nobody would find a few splintered bones amid the ash of the furnace slag.

'He didn't stay alive for all that long after we found you spying,' said Lily, grinning like an Oriental statue, rubbing her hands together.

'There was little point in prolonging his suffering, you see. Not once we knew. The fact that you'd seen us, well . . . that was enough. So he died. He had been behaving strangely. Folks will imagine he has run away in his madness and the hills or the Sioux have got him.'

'Me the same?'

'Oh, no.' Eliza bent down by him with a creaking of corsets. 'We are not fools are we sister?'

'Indeed not, sister,' replied Lily. 'We know that people know you have come here. And why you have come. There might be questions. Now poor Julius is dead, there will be no more suspicions. You will accidentally fall into the Clearwater. So sad. It's very high at present and nobody who fell into it would have a chance. So sad.'

'So very sad,' added Eliza.

'Who killed Zimmerman?' he asked, trying to buy a little time.

'Me. Why?' said Lily.

'Just so's I'd know.'

'Yes. One of the coiled probes became white hot and it kind of slipped through my hand into a certain part of his body and there he was gone. Off to play with the celestial choirs. I almost envy him.'

'Very well,' said Eliza briskly, straightening up again. 'We must get on. The night is passing and we want you out of the way quickly. Your body should be twenty miles downstream by dawn.'

'Can I not have a little . . .' began Lily, moving in closer, her high-buttoned shoes near to his head. Lifting up one foot and resting it so gently on his throat. 'Just one quick . . .'

'No!' snapped her sister. 'There must be no marks on the body that the river didn't put there. When you take him down, Matthew, you must untie his bonds. They will leave evidence on his wrists. Guard him well.'

'Sure will, Aunt Eliza,' laughed Matthew Daley, drawing his pistol and cocking it with a dramatic gesture.

'One question,' said Herne.

'A brief one,' replied Lily Sowren.

'The robberies. The mine was failing and you had to cover it up. Or what your Pa did was for nothing and Wild Rose City, your town, was going to die?'

'Correct, Mister Herne. What a loss you will be to your profession. It is indeed *our* town. We have made it and if it is to be destroyed then it is us who will destroy it.'

'That was why you stole ore? Mixed it in with the help of Zimmerman. Pretended it came from Mount Morgoth. Once smelted down there was no telling where it had come from. Easy. Damned clever.'

A foot hit him in the groin and he doubled up, nearly being sick at the pain. Only half-hearing the prim, outraged voice of Eliza Sowren.

'No such language in our presence, Mister Herne, if you please. Remember that we are ladies.'

He heard the soft noise of the shutting door, and knew that the Misses Sowren had gone, without bidding him farewell.

Matthew Daley relied on his Colt forty-five while his brother Marcus carried a weighty old Le Mat pistol. Forty-two calibre nine shot pistol chambered around a smooth-bore sixty-three calibre barrel that fired a load of buckshot as lethally as a sawn-down scatter-gun. And with about as much accuracy.

It was a comparatively unusual weapon this long after the ending of the War. Jed noticed that the saloon-keeper carried it with the hammer set for the ordinary pistol bullets.

They cut through the ties around his feet first, letting him struggle upright, leaning against the wall. Then Marcus sliced through the rope round his neck, looking to his brother for reassurance before freeing the gunslinger's hands.

'Maybe leave them be 'til we push him in. We'll bend a gun butt over his head in case he figures on swimmin' to safety. One bruise more or less won't concern nobody when they pull him out of the Clearwater in a few days.'

'Why not leave the cords on his hands? Be safer that way,' said Marcus, standing away from Herne as though he was terrified of him, even bound, with a gun held at his belly.

The sheriff shook his head. 'Nope. Better not, little brother. You all heard what Aunt Eliza said about takin' them off. She's likely to skin your back if'n she ever found you done got us all in trouble by disobeyin' her special orders.'

That was enough for Marcus Daley.

The two of them followed Herne out of the mansion and down Main Street. The wind was still rising, drowning out the thunder of the river. The ground was slippery and muddy from all the rain that had fallen, and twice Herne came close to toppling over, finding it difficult to maintain his balance in the greasy mud.

'Don't go gettin' those clothes dirty, Mister Herne,' laughed Sheriff Daley.

'They'll get washed clean soon enough,' he replied winning a grudging nod from the fatter brother. The moon broke through the scudding clouds at that moment, illuminating the pretty little town like something from a child's picture book.

'Guess you ain't a bad old boy, Jed,' muttered the lawman. 'Things could have been different, then you and me might ... Hell, no edge in figurin' on that. Let's get to it before Gawain and Joab come back from the burnin'.'

'This been going on for long, Sheriff?' asked Herne, deliberately slipping and nearly falling, remaining on his knees for a few moments before rising again, with a great staggering and lurching, nearly knocking over Marcus Daley.

'Hey, careful there, boy,' the fat man laughed. 'Don't want you goin' and bein' hurt before we kill you.'

They were soon down by the river, the noise of its rushing and crashing over the rocks making it hard to talk. Sheriff Matthew Daley called out to his brother to cut through the rope on Herne's wrists while he kept him covered. The saloon-keeper hung on to his own pistol while he fumbled for a knife.

'You asked how long this's been goin' on, Jed? Guess my aunts always been kind of strange. Specially Lily. Wow!' He laughed. 'Guess all of us could tell you tales about Aunt Lily'd make your hairs curl, boy. Ain't that right, Marcus?'

The heavily-built brother muttered his agreement while he finally got his blade free of the sheath at the side of his broad leather belt.

'Sure is, Matt. But it was when the mother lode started to run out on Mount Morgoth that they kind of went up and over the top of the world. We went along 'cos we always did. Nobody ever really stood up to them, so they didn't get the taste for losin'.'

The sheriff laughed again, standing with his back leaned against the trunk of a big tree, only a couple of paces from the edge of the water.

'Ain't that the truth, brother? Ain't that the God-damned truth. Come on there with that knife!'

'Nearly done. There!'

Jed felt the binding slip free and he brought his wrists around in front of him, pulling off the last strands of rawhide, wincing at the excruciating pain of the life flowing back into his bruised fingers. Seeing the blood clotted around his nails from the pressure of the ropes. Knowing that now was the moment to try and buy time.

'That's it, boy,' said the sheriff, motioning at him with his pistol.

'Want me to hit him with Betsy here?' grinned Marcus, waving the ponderous Le Mat.

'Guess so. Nothin' else to be said, Herne. Figure you understand that?'

'Yeah. I figure that.' His hands felt as though they were on fire and he rubbed them together, stamping his feet, watching the two Daley brothers carefully for a chance to make his move.

Sheriff Daley was standing back from the water, covering the helpless man with the Colt, waiting for his brother to knock him out and tip him into the Clearwater. The river was foaming and churning away at its banks, carrying enormous quantities of mud and stones as it raced by.

He saw Herne seem to fall, fighting for a foothold in the slippery dirt at the edge of the water. Start to slide, arms flailing, going down to his knees. Watched with a grin as Marcus stepped in to help, the pistol ready in case of a trick.

Both men were on their feet when the shootist appeared to slip again, hanging on the arm of the saloon-keeper like a drunk at closing-time.

'Get him in, Marcus!' he called to his brother, glancing around to make sure nobody else was watching the murder.

When he glanced back things had changed.

As he'd gone down on his knee Herne's right hand had dived immediately for the hilt of the bayonet, snug inside his boot. Keeping it on the blind side away from the two Daleys. Pretending to have difficulty in standing up and grabbing at Marcus Daley for support. Once he felt the rough cloth of the man's coat in his hand there was a rush of exultation, knowing that it was going to work.

The bayonet had been his since he first joined Quantrill and his group of bloody guerillas near the start of the War. He cherished it, keeping it polished and honed. The edge sharp enough to shave with, the point as keen as a needle.

It slithered in between the fourth and fifth ribs on the left side of the man's chest. Jed gave it a savage twist and pulled it free, dropping it to the ground. It had done what he wanted of it.

Marcus Daley never really knew what had happened, and he slipped away from life, still puzzled. There was the feeling of a slight blow. No sensation of being cut at all. A dull pain in the middle of his body. Wetness and warmth over his stomach and thighs. A great weakness.

Herne took the gun from his relaxing fingers as easily as from a young child, pushing the dying man to one side. Daley's legs no longer supported him as the blood poured from his burst heart and he fell forwards, landing head-first in the Clearwater.

The body was whirled away, tossing and turning like a hewn log, spinning away on the whirling pools and eddies of the flooded river. Finally becoming caught up with some rubbish several miles downstream and drifting into a backwater.

The rotting corpse was never found.

The last that Matthew Daley saw of his brother was the body flailing into the Clearwater. There wasn't time for any kind of goodbyes. The lawman's eyes were held by the big pistol that had miraculously appeared in Herne's fist. One moment the shootist was helpless, about to be clubbed and drowned. Next moment Matthew's brother was dead and he was facing the barrel of a pistol.

He didn't understand it.

Died not understanding it, his flesh ripped apart by four carefully placed shots from the Le Mat, never even having the time to fire back.

Herne threw his body in the river as well, then went on into Wild Rose to wait for the Sowren brothers. It was going well.

CHAPTER ELEVEN

There were five shots left in the Le Mat and Herne also had the sheriff's Colt forty-five in his holster. Eleven bullets in all. Plus a dozen that he'd taken from Matthew Daley's belt before tipping his body into the turbulent waters of the river.

Two Sowren boys left.

Then Eliza and Lily.

Herne figured he had the odds fractionally on his side now. There was the important factor that he knew they were alive and they believed he was dead. But that tipping of the balance wouldn't last for ever.

Miss Eliza began to suspect it.

When the nephews didn't return in half an hour from their task of executing the shootist, then she suspected it.

She stood by the window of the great mansion, looking down over the sleeping town, her fingers knotting and tangling with each other. Her mouth a grim line of steel beneath her questing nose. Sighing to herself as she began to realise that the tall man with the greying hair had undone everything that mattered in her life. In her sister's life. Her father's, everything.

Eliza turned away to the room, luxurious, the original oil-paintings from Europe on the walls, illuminated by the gentle glow of the lamps. The expensive glass and china on the polished table and the gleaming silver plate and cutlery.

'Lily,' she called. 'Come here, will you. There are some things that we must do.'

Jed guessed that the noise of the shooting would have been totally muffled by the pounding waters, and he stalked away towards the main trail in from the mine, confident that nobody in the town of Wild Rose knew that he was free and on the scent of bloody vengeance.

The Sowrens must have finished their task of removing Zimmerman's body. It wouldn't take long to clear other men from the furnace room at Mount Morgoth. Certainly if you were the sons of Eliza Sowren it would be absurdly simple. Then to open the great doors and slide in the corpse, wincing away from the white heat inside. There might be the momentary stench of roasting flesh in the air above the smelting plant, but the stink of the chemicals would soon overpower it.

The moon still rode high in the Dakota sky, the few scattered clouds disappearing, leaving a cool night with a rising wind that continued to tug at the topmost branches of the trees. Jed stepped cautiously along until he reached a thick grove of bushes, close in to the rutted trail. He crouched down, out of sight, and waited. Knowing that it wasn't going to take long.

In the house, Lily was getting hastily dressed, while her sister waited impatiently below. Out back, by the wall of the silent graveyard, servants were busy loading cans of liquid into the light rig. A horse, already harnessed, stamped its hooves nervously, scenting a strange tautness in the air.

It was difficult for Herne to catch the noise of movement above the sound of the river and the sighing of the wind, but he finally heard hooves, clattering quickly towards him.

In the darkness among the trees it would be easy to miss a shot at the men. Fatally easy. Moonlight did strange things to angles and distances when you were shooting, and Jed couldn't afford any mistakes.

It wasn't a time for being sentimental about animals.

As the two riders came round the nearest bend, moving at a fast trot, he readied himself. A gun in each hand. Herne wasn't completely ambidextrous, but he was as good with his left hand as most men were with their right.

Joab and Gawain were in high spirits. Now that the dangerously nervous manager was dead and fried to a crisp, and that murdering shootist was bobbing wetly down the Clearwater, the road ahead lay straight and clear for them. Nothing was going to stop them now.

'Hold it, you sons of bitches!!' yelled Jedediah Herne, stepping out of the bushes directly in front of them, like an Apache shaman leaping from a cloud of smoke to terrify even the stoutest of hearts.

'Jesus Christ!!' screamed Joab Sowren, fumbling for his rifle.

His brother, Gawain didn't shout anything at all. He was too busy fighting his horse that had reared up in terror at the frightening appearance of the man, right under its hooves.

Calm as if he was at early morning practice, Herne pumped three bullets into each animal, using the Colt in his left hand. Feeling the pistol buck and kick against his wrist. Seeing in the silver light the black splodges of blood that burst out on the chests on both horses, the impact of the bullets knocking them over in the slippery mud.

Joab was so concerned with trying for his Winchester that he was slow in reacting. As his horse rolled under him, he never managed to get his boots clear of the stirrups and was trapped by the leg. A snapping sound and a lance of fiery pain telling him that the bones were crushed by the weight of the animal. From where he lay, he couldn't reach his gun, and the tossing of the dying creature's head prevented him even seeing the man that had attacked them.

Gawain was luckier and quicker.

Jumping sideways as the horse fell, landing in a crouch, his hand going for the pistol at his belt. There had been a time when Gawain Sowren had been fast with a hand-gun. As a younger man he'd practised a whole lot, in the rolling country out beyond the cemetery. But that had been long years back. Though he was only about the same age as Jed, maybe a year or so older, his years had been soft and easy.

Herne's years had been long and hard. Keeping the edge that Sowren had long lost.

Jed dropped the empty Colt in the dirt by his feet, thumbing back the Le Mat, snapping off a quick shot at the kneeling man. Seeing the effect it had.

Gawain screamed once, high and thin, like a stallion being gelded, and his arms flew up and wide as if he'd seen a long-lost friend and was readying himself to greet him. But the expression on his face was one of agony, not greeting. The bullet had hit him in the chest, just above the breastbone, sending him slumping back, rolling in the mud. Trying to scream again but blood from his torn lungs flooded into his throat and mouth, choking him.

He clapped his hands to the wound, pressing as hard as he could, attempting to force the pain away. As he tried to sit up, Herne shot him through the centre of the head, the forty-two ripping away most of his nose, opening the middle of his face like a butcher's cleaver. Angling up sideways and back, forcing one eye from its socket where it dangled on Sowren's cheek, still attached by the gristle of the muscle and the optic nerve.

The distorted bullet mangled a chunk from the middle-aged man's brain before finally stopping its progress. Gawain Sowren died blinded and alone, face down in dirt, his fingers clawing for a handful of earth. That was all the birthright that death left him.

There were three bullets left in the Le Mat, and one son to kill.

Joab Sowren was struggling for his life, his brain threatening to slip away from his control into a helpless hysteria. One moment all had been well and they'd been riding along happily, pushing on to report their success to their mother and to Aunt Lily. Then an appalling horror had erupted among them.

His brother was dead. He knew that. The two bullets, the scream and that awful choking, bubbling sound. And now it was his turn. He could feel his broken leg crushed by the horse. Even see the shattered fragments of white bone sticking through the torn cloth of his trousers. His horse was finally still, blood tumbling from its wounds and pattering on the dirt. Flooding down the slope of the trail, stark in the moonlight, looking like spilled ink.

'Herne?' he yelled, voice cracking. 'That you, Herne? Is it?'

There was no answer. Jed was waiting quietly, unable to see beyond the corpse of the horse, whether the man had a gun in his hand or not. In the middle of the action, amid the noise of the bullets and the drifting clouds of powder smoke, he thought he'd heard the clean crack of a bone breaking, but he wasn't sure. Not sure enough to want to risk his life on it.

'Herne? Do this mean what I think it means?'

From out of the darkness there floated a voice as cold as a midnight tomb.

'It do.'

'My leg's broke, Herne,' called Joab.

'What the Hell d'you want me to do? Come and nurse you?'

'You killed Gawain?'

'Yeah.'

'And Matthew and Marcus? Must have if'n you're here and alive.'

'You figure good. Just like a damned banker, Sowren. Even a crooked banker.'

At that moment, Eliza and Lily were sitting in their withdrawing room, a half mile away up the hill, waiting patiently. Not wanting to be too precipitate. Eliza had ruled that they would wait until half-past four. If nobody had returned by then they would assume that all was lost and they would act accordingly.

They both knew what they must do.

That had been agreed among the family many years back. Even though none of them had ever imagined that it would come to it. None of them had ever imagined that there was a man around like Herne the Hunter.

'Let me alone, Herne.'

'You're wastin' breath, Sowren. Man as close to death as you are should be makin' peace with his gods, not whining on about livin'.'

'I'll pay you, Herne. Thousand dollars.'

'Forget it, Sowren.'

'Ten thousand dollars. That's a lot of money.'

'Sure is. And I got me plenty of life to think on the way I earned it. Thanks a lot, Mister Sowren, but I guess not.'

'Anything . . .'

'You don't need to offer that much, Sowren. All I want

is one bullet through your head. That'll do me. Kind of pay off some scores for all the men you and your murderin' family butchered in all those robberies.'

'Wasn't my idea.' Joab was still fighting to free himself, but the dead weight of the horse was too much. At first shock had eased off the pain from the broken leg, but now it was inching back in. Tearing at him like the claws of a wild animal.

'I know that, Sowren. It was your mother and her crazy sister. They're goin' to get theirs too, not that I go much for killin' women. But I'm real prepared to make an exception for those two.'

By now he was beginning to suspect that Sowren wasn't armed. Or was so badly hurt he couldn't get at his pistol. But a suspicion wasn't enough to go walking up on, and he started to move around, skirting the grove of bushes that had first hidden him. Moving silent as a Chiricahua warrior, setting down each foot as carefully as if he was treading on eggshells.

At last he could see partly behind the corpse of the horse, settled in the mud. The banker was there, struggling to lift his head and see where Herne was.

'Where are you? Damn it! Don't just go off and leave me here. I'll die.'

There was no answer.

Jed stepped in closer to him. Closing the gap. Watching the man's hands, seeing they couldn't reach the holstered gun trapped under him.

'Come on!! Help!!! Help!!!'

Sowren's control was going as he realised that he'd been left with his broken leg. It could be a day or more until anyone came along and found him. By then he'd be dead from pain and shock.

'Don't leave me,' he whimpered. 'Help me. Please.

Mama. Help Joab. Help me, Mama. Please help me.' His voice had dropped so low that Herne could hardly catch it, and the middle-aged banker was beginning to cry.

'Not fair, Mama. Please.'

In his morbid terror, he hardly even noticed the cold of the muzzle of the Le Mat against his muddied hair.

'So long,' said Herne, in a pleasant conversational voice, squeezing the trigger once.

At the crown of the head the hair hadn't got wet from the muddy earth, and the explosion of the pistol at point blank range set fire to it. Filling Herne's nostrils with the smell of scorched hair. But it sizzled for only a moment.

Jed had aimed for a little behind the right ear, so that the bullet would bury itself in the middle of the brain. It was surprising how you could shoot a man through the head and not kill him. Herne recalled a dance-hall girl in Natchez, or could it have been Dallas? A girl who'd fired two shots from an over-and-under Deringer through her head and failed to kill herself. Both bullets had passed through without doing any fatal damage.

But the shots had scarred her face, taking away part of her jaw and most of her teeth. As soon as she was free from hospital she'd gone on down to the river and drowned herself.

'Natchez,' he said to himself, remembering.

Standing up from the twitching corpse of Joab Sowren, wiping shards of bone from his sleeve, specks of blood and pink brain from the back of his hand.

Three nephews and two sons dead.

Herne looked up at the moon sinking slowly down towards the distant hills. The night was nearly over. He stood close to the trail and reloaded the Colt, sticking it in his belt. Glancing down at the two corpses.

'Well,' he said to himself, 'I guess it's about time to go join the ladies.'

CHAPTER TWELVE

Because of her bulk, Lily found it hard work scurrying about the dark, silent town, carrying the cans. Pouring out the liquid around the walls and doors of the houses and stores. Splattering the saloon with it. Gagging at the heavy smell. Wrinkling her nose with distaste as some of it splashed on her pink dress. Though it was still cool, she was sweating from her exertions.

Eliza also struggled with her labours. Despite her skinny build, she was strong for such an old woman, heaving out the cans, and rolling them along to pour them out where they would do most good.

At one point she straightened up with a groan of discomfort, putting both hands in the small of her back. Feeling the wind ruffling the silver hair, and she smiled.

'Best kind of wind. Do most of the work for us,' she said. Even though there wasn't anyone there to hear her, alone among the shadows.

She checked her purse to make sure she was carrying the box of lucifers to ignite the fires. And plenty of brown wrapping paper to make certain that gallons and gallons of oil caught properly. Despite the recent rains, the wood of the buildings was dry and painted. With this wind it wouldn't take too long for the entire town to go up in flames.

'We made it, Papa,' she muttered as she climbed back into the rig for more oil. 'And we can destroy it.'

Eliza Sowren seemed to be acting quite rationally. In her own mind there was nothing wrong with what she was doing. Nor was there any doubt in Lily's mind. They had agreed it was right and so it *was* right. It had been all along. The only way to save the town had been to steal and murder so that the mine would not die. Now all of that was over, spoiled for them by that wretched Herne. She looked again in her purse, making sure the little pocket pistol was safe and snug. If all went well, she would be able to make Wild Rose City into a fitting funeral pyre for Mister Jedediah Herne.

Eliza and Lily Sowren were, of course, quite mad.

Jed smelled the oil before he reached the first building of the town. His initial thought was that someone had spilled a can of it, or that someone's storage tank was leaking. But it was very strong. Riding over the top of everything else, tugging at his nostrils despite the wind, now rising to near a gale.

Then there was the flickering of a light a couple of hundred yards ahead of him. And the bits of the puzzle clicked into place.

'Oh, Jesus! They're setting fire to the whole damned place,' he said, wonderingly.

The first glimmer of orange light was growing even as he stood and looked at it. There were others. Seeming to spring up everywhere. Eliza had made her plans well, making sure that she and Lily were able to light nearly twenty blazes, most of them tucked away around the backs of properties. So that there was no chance of any of them being seen.

He caught a glimpse of someone moving, near the front of the saloon, and he drew the Colt, wondering whether to risk a shot. Even in the moonlight, he was sure that he recognised the tall, angular frame of Eliza Sowren.

But there were more important things to consider. With

the wind set the way it was, it could well sweep through Wild Rose City in a matter of minutes, leaping from neat frame house to neat frame house. Devouring the entire town in flames.

Already, as he stood and considered what to do, he could see the fire beginning to gain an unstoppable hold. There was no way of knowing how many people in the town were actively involved in the robberies. Probably quite a few of them. But with the Sowrens dead, they would be safe.

'Fire!' he shouted. 'Fire!! Fire!!!' Snapping off all six shots from the Peacemaker into the night air, the noise booming about him.

Then he began to run. Digging his heels into the muddy street, powering his way towards where he'd seen Eliza. She must have heard the shots and would know what that meant. And Lily must be around as well.

Windows were sliding up as he ran, voices calling out. Shouting. A woman screaming. For a hideous moment it brought back to him August twenty-first, eighteen sixty-three and the fire-death of Lawrence, Kansas when Quantrill and his men massacred one hundred and forty-two men, women and children.

He'd been there, helping with the killing and burning. Now there was the chance to set the scores back a little.

By the time Jed reached *The Rich Nugget* saloon, it was well ablaze. It seemed as if the whole of Wild Rose was burning away, the flames leaping from house to house with a dreadful ferocity, carried by the strong wind. The air was filled with glowing sparks whirling by, and his ears rang with the crashing of timber and the breaking of glass.

Men were shouting and he saw a child dash out into the street ahead of him, its nightdress flaring as it ran. A man appeared and flung a blanket over the child, dowsing the flames.

Everywhere people were pouring out of buildings. Some to stand and weep. Some to shout for water. For a bucket chain to be organised. For anything that would help.

Three times questions were called out to Herne, and he replied, telling them what had happened, knowing the words would spread around the doomed town almost as quickly as the flames. Telling them that the ladies had done it, as a final revenge on the world, once their wickedness was discovered.

Knowing that it would not take long for them to come seeking revenge from the Misses Sowren. A revenge that Herne felt should come from him and from him alone.

The fire had been started around the rear of the saloon, and had raced through the building, leaping from dry painted wall to ceiling to floor to drapes and furniture. It could only be a matter of moments before the shingled roof collapsed. As Herne stood watching the awesome scene, he saw some of the roofing timbers being whirled away into the air by the furnace-heat, carrying their flames with them to start a dozen new blazes.

But where were the ladies?

He was sure he'd seen Eliza close by the saloon, but there had been no sign of Lily. He decided that he would walk around the block, guessing that they must have had a wagon to carry all the oil.

As soon as he stepped from the brightness of Main Street he heard the crack of a small hand-gun, and flinched away as a bullet dug splinters of white wood from the wall close to his head. It was pretty shooting in poor light with a small gun.

'Nice try, Ma'am,' he called out, the Le Mat ready in his fist. Dropping to one knee and scanning the dim alley for a glimpse of the woman. Suddenly, away beyond the blazing building, he heard the crack of a whip and saw a wagon race across, heading up the hill. Towards the Sowren mansion. Driven by a hunched, grotesquely fat figure, the pale face turned in his direction. It was past so quickly that there was no chance of a shot at Lily as she flogged the horse out of sight.

That meant it was Eliza with the gun.

Behind him, the inhabitants of Wild Rose were nearly all out in the streets, like ghosts in their night-clothes, seeking revenge. Calling out, a growing anger from the lunatic fringe.

'Hang the witches!!!' he heard. Or was it 'Bitches'? It could have been both.

'Mister Herne!!' came the cold voice from the shadows. 'I am over here.'

It was a back door to the saloon. Either side of it were windows, splintering in the heat, showing the bright squares of flame. The room beyond the door must be an inferno of heat. There were some boxes piled by the door, and Herne knew that Eliza Sowren must be behind them. They were mainly of thin board.

The Le Mat had three bullets left.

He took a chance and fired two of them through the boxes, both about the place he'd reckoned that a woman's breastbone would be. About nine inches apart, gambling that Eliza would be too much the lady to do anything like hitching up her skirt and crouching down in the dirt of the back alley.

The gamble paid off.

There wasn't a scream. More of a muffled groan. And she appeared.

The pistol still in her right hand, the other pressed to her stomach, where dark blood oozed between her gloved fingers. He'd forgotten just how tall she was. In an ordinary woman the one shot would have certainly killed her, going clean through the heart. But it was too low. Barely above the sash around her waist, buried deep in her stomach. It would probably kill her in the end.

For Jed, that wasn't enough.

'You win, Mister Herne,' she called out, her voice still strong. 'You have won, and we have lost. Who would have thought it?'

She half-turned for a moment at the crashing sound of beams breaking off and cascading inside the shell of the saloon in a burst of red and gold sparks. Then turned back to face him.

'The mine was dead. Now the town is dead. We are finished, Mister Herne.' She paused as if she was gathering strength, eyeing him across the narrow street, the fires all around making it light as day, and he recoiled from the unflinching malevolence in her gaze. Realising what a very remarkable woman she had been.

Still was, even so close to the ending.

'And you are finished with us!!!' she screamed, levelling the Deringer at him.

Eliza Sowren never got to squeeze the trigger of the little gun.

The last bullet from the Le Mat took her through the bridge of that amazingly bony nose, smashing on into her brain, killing her instantly. To Herne it was as though a flower of deepest crimson had bloomed in the centre of her face, the petals spreading down over her mouth and across the purple dress. The gun fell from her fingers and she staggered back against the door of *The Rich Nugget*.

Which opened as if a servant had been inside waiting for her entrance, welcoming her into the maelstrom of fire beyond.

The body toppled backwards and vanished in the silver heat of the flames. Immediately afterwards there was another splintering and more timbers from the saloon roof fell in on top of her, burying the corpse.

Herne sniffed and stood there for a moment, looking at the mighty wreckage all around him. Eliza Sowren had done her work well.

All that now remained was her sister.

Nobody had heard the noise of the shooting above the other sounds of the dying township. He glanced out again into Main Street, seeing that the fire was now raging through the length and breadth of Wild Rose. Men had formed a hasty and ineffective bucket chain down near the Clearwater, but they might as well have tried to stop a bullet with a wet neckerchief.

Others were battling to save some of their furniture and possessions, throwing down beds and books from upstairs windows. Women shepherded weeping children away from the blaze towards the surrounding woods.

A few men were standing together arguing furiously. One of them holding a loop of hemp rope in his fists, shaking it angrily towards the top of the hill.

Jed ducked back into the alley, crouching into a loping run past Eliza's funeral pyre, turning left and heading up towards the mansion by the graveyard.

Towards Lily Sowren.

Several times in that climb he was forced to slip aside from piles of burning embers and wood as walls and roofs crashed down about his ears. Nobody was bothering about the backs of the properties, all the action coming in Main Street. It only took him a couple of minutes to reach the main gates of the Sowren house, staring behind him once to see the total devastation of the town. It seemed that every single building was ablaze, the light dazzling in the dark of early morning. The sparks and smoke rose in a mighty red-tinted column hundreds of feet into the air, being finally dispersed by the wind.

By the iron gates of the big house, there was a chattering gaggle of servants, all huddled together. All in their night-clothes. One of them recognised Herne and came running over.

'Miss Lily, Mister Herne. We fear she's come over all strange, Mister Herne.'

'Why?'

'She come back a few minutes ago and ordered us all from the house. Had a gun with her, she did.'

'Smelled of lamp-oil, Sir,' added a girl, her eyes pools of fear in a white face.

'Then we saw the fires, and we think she has a mind to burn us all out.'

Herne nodded. 'Then all keep clear. Wait. You,' pointing to the middle-aged man who had been the butler.

'Sir?'

'See to my horse from the stable. And I want my guns and possessions removed from the house. Now, before it's too damned late.'

'Sir, I don't think Miss Eliza would like to hear such language.'

Jed grabbed the servant by the shoulder with fingers as tight as iron chains. 'That bloody-minded bitch is dead and will hear nothing more this side of eternity. Do as I tell you. I have to see Miss Lily.'

He stalked away from them. Leaving a shocked silence behind as if he had spat in the face of a visiting preacher.

In the hall he stopped and sniffed. Was there the hint of smoke?

He looked up the sweeping staircase, and he saw clear evidence that the Sowren mansion was not to escape the general conflagration that was destroying Wild Rose City. There was indeed smoke, creeping in coiled tendrils along the landing, beginning to pour down the stairs like a murky river. And there was the distant crackle of flames, somewhere in the upper reaches of the big house.

He guessed where the old woman would have gone. Back to her lair like a dying animal.

To her own locked room.

Halfway up the stairs, Herne paused, realising that he had no further ammunition and only the empty Le Mat pistol. But he had not used the scatter-gun barrel of the unique gun. It was the work of a moment to alter the hammer nose, making sure the nipple of the percussion cap was standing in place.

The smoke grew thicker as he walked to the top of the staircase, going to the right where Lily Sowren had her den. Stopping again when he was outside the heavy oaken door. Hearing the faint sound of someone weeping.

'No,' he said to himself. 'Not weeping. The bitch is laughing!'

Holding the Le Mat steady in his right hand, Herne reached out with his left and gently... very gently... turned the ornamental brass knob of the door. Certain that he would find it locked.

It was open.

'Come in,' said a voice, heavy with drink. 'That must be naughty Jedediah that's spoiled everything. Nobody else would care to ... I mean dare to come in like that.'

He remembered the servants had mentioned a gun. After all their killings, the sisters were so deep in blood that to kill him would only be another entry in the long column of butchery.

'Come in, do. Let us have an end to this. Eliza is dead is she not?'

He slowly edged the door open, suddenly seeing a discarded Deringer, like the one Eliza had carried, on the carpet of the bedroom.

'She is.'

'I knew it. Where?'

'By the saloon. It fell on her.'

There was a bellow of laughter from within. 'That's rich! Stupid, dried-up, drained, saggin' old whore! That's fuckin' rich, Herne. Fuckin' rich!'

Behind him the noise of flames was growing louder every moment and the smell of smoke thicker in his nostrils. There wasn't much time. But he was determined not to leave it open at the end. Not for Zimmerman. And the rest.

He pushed the door open, and stopped, stricken by what he saw.

Lily Sowren was naked on her bed. The great rolls of her fat cascading about her like a stranded whale. Her breasts sagged to her belly, the nipples buried in wrinkled skin. She lay with her legs apart, her hands busy between her thighs. The room stank of whisky and the heavy ruttish scent of her body.

And beneath her on the stained coverlet. Beneath her. Around her. On top of her. A mountain of pictures. Hand-tinted daguerreotypes. All showing the same thing. Men. Mainly young, from what Herne saw in that glance. All naked. Each one revealing himself to the camera in a way that Herne did not believe a normal man could do.

'You like what you see, Jedediah. Come and love me a little. I'm old and ill and terrified and a bit in drink, dear boy. Come to me.'

He was disgusted.

Almost without knowing he did it, Herne the Hunter

pulled the trigger of the Le Mat, sending the charge of buckshot ripping through her naked body. Tearing into her breasts and stomach, punching a massive hole in her soft, old flesh. Blood gouted from her, soaking over the pictures, pouring through on the bed, dripping to the floor.

He turned away and left her without a single backwards glance. Leaving the room. The house.

Leaving Wild Rose City, with his guns and his possessions and his horse.

Nobody tried to stop him and he didn't check the stallion until they were on the crest of the hill to the east. The sky had lightened with the promise of the false dawn, and he looked at the smouldering smoking ruins of the beautiful town, with the river running on ceaselessly behind it.

And he thought at that moment of a song that Lily Sowren had loved. One she said was very new. A friend had got it for her from another friend.

'*Darling, I am growing old,*
Silver threads among the gold
Shine upon my brow today;
Life is fading fast away.'

After that thought, Herne didn't look back again. There wasn't any point.

THE END

HERNE THE HUNTER 8 : CROSS-DRAW
by John J. McLaglen

Herne was upon him. A grip like a vice clamped down on his right arm and something that felt like falling rock thudded against his jaw. A fire shot through him as a knee was rammed between his legs and he knew he was falling backwards, knew his mouth was open wide and that what he could hear was the sound of himself screaming. Screaming with pain like some foolish kid . . .

Trouble was brewing when rival ranch owners started using the town of Liberation as their private battleground. When it started, the war between the Double C and the Broken Bar was a cold one. When Herne the Hunter pinned on the deputy Marshal's shield, all of a sudden the war got red hot . . .

0 552 10788 3—**60p**